After handing the letter op
sheet of paper from the envel
snapshot fluttered to the floor.

Zack stooped to retrieve the photo. "A newborn?" he asked, showing it to me.

"I would think so." The baby in the picture looked no more than a day or two old.

Zack flipped over the photo to reveal a date. "Nearly fifty years ago," he said.

As I began to read the letter, I quickly realized the contents were indeed meant for Lupe. "Oh, my!"

Acclaim for the Anastasia Pollack Crafting Mysteries

Assault with a Deadly Glue Gun

"Crafty cozies don't get any better than this hilarious confection...Anastasia is as deadpan droll as Tina Fey's Liz Lemon, and readers can't help cheering as she copes with caring for a host of colorful characters." – *Publishers Weekly* (starred review)

"Winston has hit a homerun with this hilarious, laugh-until-your-sides-hurt tale. Oddball characters, uproariously funny situations, and a heroine with a strong sense of irony will delight fans of Janet Evanovich, Jess Lourey, and Kathleen Bacus. May this be the first of many in Winston's Anastasia Pollack Crafting Mystery series." – *Booklist* (starred review)

"A comic tour de force...Lovers of funny mysteries, outrageous puns, self-deprecating humor, and light romance will all find something here." – *ForeWord Magazine* (Book-of-the-Year nominee)

"North Jersey's more mature answer to Stephanie Plum. Funny, gutsy, and determined, Anastasia has a bright future in the planned series." – *Kirkus Reviews*

"...a delightful romp through the halls of who-done-it." – *The Star-Ledger*

"Make way for Lois Winston's promising new series...I'll be eagerly awaiting the next installment in this thoroughly delightful series." – *Mystery Scene Magazine*

"...once you read the first few pages of Lois Winston's first-in-series whodunit, you're hooked for the duration..." – *Bookpage*

"...madcap but tough-as-nails, no holds barred plot and main character...a step above the usual crafty cozy." – *The Mystery Reader*

"...Anastasia is, above all, a JERSEY girl..., and never, ever mess with one of them. I can't wait 'til the next book in this series..." – *Suspense Magazine*

"Anastasia is as crafty as Martha Stewart, as feisty as Stephanie Plum, and as resourceful as Kinsey Millhone." – Mary Kennedy, author of the Talk Radio Mysteries

"Fans of Stephanie Plum will love Lois Winston's cast of quirky, laughable, and loveable characters. *Assault with a Deadly Glue Gun* is clever and thoroughly entertaining—a must read!" – Brenda Novak, *New York Times* best-selling author

"What a treat—I can't stop laughing! Witty, wise, and delightfully clever, Anastasia is going to be your new best friend. Her mysterious adventures are irresistible—you'll be glued to the page!" – Hank Phillippi Ryan, Agatha, Anthony, and Macavity award-winning author

"You think you've got trouble? Say hello to Anastasia Pollack, who also happens to be queen of the one-liners. Funny, funny, funny— this is a series you don't want to miss!" – Kasey Michaels, *USA Today* best-selling author

Death by Killer Mop Doll

"Anastasia is a crafting Stephanie Plum, surrounded by characters sure to bring chuckles as she careens through the narrative, crossing paths with the detectives assigned to the case and snooping around to solve it." – *Booklist*

"Several crafts projects, oodles of laughs and an older, more centered version of Stephanie Plum." – *Kirkus Reviews*

"In Winston's droll second cozy featuring crafts magazine editor Anastasia Pollack...readers who relish the offbeat will be rewarded." – *Publishers Weekly*

"...a *30 Rock* vibe...Winston turns out another lighthearted amateur sleuth investigation. Laden with one-liners, Anastasia's second outing (after *Assault With a Deadly Glue Gun*) points to another successful series in the works." – *Library Journal*

"Winston...plays for plenty of laughs...while letting Anastasia shine as a risk-taking investigator who doesn't always know when to quit." – *Alfred Hitchcock Mystery Magazine*

Revenge of the Crafty Corpse

"Winston peppers the twisty and slightly edgy plot with humor and plenty of craft patterns. Fans of craft mysteries will like this, of course, but so will those who enjoy the smart and snarky humor of Janet Evanovich, Laura Levine, and Laura DeSilverio." – *Booklist*

"Winston's entertaining third cozy plunges Anastasia into a surprisingly fraught stew of jealousy, greed, and sex..." and a "Sopranos-worthy lineup of eccentric character..." – *Publishers Weekly*

"Winston provides a long-suffering heroine, amusing characters, a...good mystery and a series of crafting projects featuring cloth yo-yos." – *Kirkus Reviews*

"A fun addition to a series that keeps getting stronger." – *Romantic Times Magazine*

"Chuckles begin on page one and the steady humor sustains a comedic crafts cozy, the third (after *Death by Killer Mop Doll*)... Recommend for Chris Grabenstein ("John Ceepak" series) and Jess Lourey readers." – *Library Journal*

"You'll be both surprised and entertained by this terrific mystery. I can't wait to see what happens in the Pollack household next." – *Suspense Magazine*

"The book has what a mystery should...It moves along at a good pace...Like all good sleuths, Anastasia pieces together what others don't...The book has a fun twist...and it's clear that Anastasia, the everyday woman who loves crafts and desserts, and has a complete hottie in pursuit, will return to solve another murder and offer more crafts tips..." – *Star-Ledger*

Decoupage Can Be Deadly

"*Decoupage Can Be Deadly* is the fourth in the Anastasia Pollock Crafting Mysteries by Lois Winston. And it's the best one yet. More, please!" – *Suspense Magazine*

"What a great cozy mystery series. One of the reasons this series stands out for me as a great one is the absolutely great cast of characters. Every single character in these books is awesomely quirky and downright hilarious. This series is a true laugh out loud read!" – Books Are Life–Vita Libri

"This is one of these series that no matter what, I'm going to be laughing my way through a comedy of errors as our reluctant heroine sets a course of action to find a killer while contending with her eccentrically dysfunctional family. This adventure grabs you immediately delivering a fast-paced and action-filled drama that doesn't let up from the first page to the surprising conclusion." – Dru's Book Musings

"Lois Winston's reluctant amateur sleuth Anastasia Pollack is back in another wild romp." – The Book Breeze

A Stitch to Die For

"*A Stitch to Die For* is the fifth in the *Anastasia Pollack Crafting Mysteries* by Lois Winston. If you're a reader who enjoys a well-plotted mystery and loves to laugh, don't miss this one!" – *Suspense Magazine*

Scrapbook of Murder

"This is one of the best books in this delightfully entertaining whodunit and I hope there are more stories in the future." – Dru's Book Musings

"*Scrapbook of Murder* is a perfect example of what mysteries are all about—deft plotting, believable characters, well-written dialogue, and a satisfying, logical ending. I loved it!" – *Suspense Magazine*

"I read an amazing book recently, y'all — *Scrapbook of Murder* by Lois Winston, #6 in the Anastasia Pollack Crafting Mysteries. All six novels and three novellas in the series are Five Star reads." – Jane Reads

"Well written, with interesting characters." – Laura's Interests

"...a quick read, with humour, a good mystery and very interesting characters!" – Verietats

Drop Dead Ornaments

"I always forget how much I love this series until I read the next one and I fall in love all over again..." – Dru's Book Musings

"*Drop Dead Ornaments* is a delightful addition to the Anastasia Pollack Crafting Mystery series. More, please!" – *Suspense Magazine*

"I love protagonist Anastasia Pollack. She's witty and funny, and she can be sarcastic at times...A great whodunit, with riotous twists and turns, *Drop Dead Ornaments* was a fast, exciting read that really kept me on my toes." – Lisa Ks Book reviews

"*Drop Dead Ornaments* is such a fantastic book...I adore

Anastasia! She's clever, likable, fun to read about, and easy to root for." – Jane Reads

"...readers will be laughing continually at the antics of Anastasia and clan in *Drop Dead Ornaments*." – The Avid Reader

"I love this series! Not only is Anastasia a 'crime magnet,' she is hilarious and snarky, a delight to read about and a dedicated friend." – Mallory Heart's Cozies

"It is always a nice surprise when something I am reading has a tie in to actual news or events that are happening in the present moment. I don't want to spoil a major plot secret, but the timing could not have been better...Be prepared for a dysfunctional cast of quirky characters." – Laura's Interests

"This is a Tour de Force of a Murder/Mystery." – A Wytch's Book Review

"Lois Winston's cozy craft mystery *Drop Dead Ornaments* is an enjoyable...roller-coaster ride, with secrets and clues tugging the reader this way and that, and gentle climbs and drops of suspense and revelation to keep them reading." – Here's How It Happened

"...a light-hearted cozy mystery with lots of energy and definitely lots of action and interaction between characters." – Curling Up By the Fire

Handmade Ho-Ho Homicide
"Handmade Ho-Ho Homicide" is a laugh-out-loud, well plotted mystery, from a real pro! A ho-ho hoot!" – *Suspense Magazine*

"Merry *Crises*! Lois Winston has brought back Anastasia's delightful first-person narrative of family, friends, dysfunction, and murder, and made it again very entertaining! Anastasia's clever quips, fun stories, and well-deserved digs kept me smiling, and reading the many funny parts to my husband...does that count as two thumbs up in one?" – *Kings River Life Magazine*

"Once again, the author knows how to tell a story that immediately grabbed my attention and I couldn't put this book down until the last page was read.... This was one of the best books in this delightfully lovable series and I can't wait to see what exciting adventures await Anastasia and her friends." – Dru's Book Musings

"This was such a fun quick read. I can't wait to read more of this series." – A Chick Who Reads

"The story had me on the edge of my seat the entire time." – 5 Stars, Baroness Book Trove

"Christmas, cozy mystery, craft, how can I not love this book? Humor, twists and turns, adorable characters make this story truly engaging from the first to the last page." – LibriAmoriMiei

"Take a murder mystery, add some light-hearted humor and weird characters, sprinkle some snow and what you get is *Handmade Ho-Ho Homicide*—a perfect Christmas Cozy read." –5 stars, The Book Decoder

A Sew Deadly Cruise

"*A Sew Deadly Cruise* is absolutely delightful, and I was sorry when it was over. I devoured every word!" – *Suspense* Magazine

"Engaging Drama! Brilliant! *A Sew Deadly Cruise* earns 5/5 Upgraded Cabins. Winston's witty first-person narrative and banter keeps me a fan. Loved it!" –*Kings River Life* Magazine

"The author knows how to tell a story with great aplomb and when all was said and done, this was one fantastic whodunit that left me craving for more thrilling adventures." – Dru's Book Musings

"The combo of investigating and fun makes for a great read. The author does a good job of keeping the killer a secret. Overall a fun read that cozy fans are sure to enjoy." – Books a Plenty Book Reviews

"Winston has a gift for writing complicated cozy mysteries while entertaining and educating." – Here's How it Happened

Stitch, Bake, Die!

"Lois Winston has crafted another clever tale...with a backdrop of cross stitching, buttercream, bribery, sabotage, rumors, and murder...with vivid descriptions, witty banter, and clever details leading to an exciting and shocking conclusion. All making for a page-turner experience to delight cozy fans." – *Kings River Life* magazine

"...a crème de la crème of a cozy read." – Brianne's Book Reviews

"...a well-plotted mystery that takes the term 'crafty old lady' to new heights." – Mysteries with Character

"This story is fast-paced with wacky characters, a fun resort setting, and a puzzling mystery to solve." – Nancy J. Cohen, author of the Bad Hair Day Mysteries

"Lots of action, a bevy of quirky characters, and a treasure trove of secrets add up to another fine read from Lois Winston." – Maggie Toussaint, author of the Seafood Caper Mysteries, Lindsey & Ike Mysteries, and the Dreamwalker Mysteries

"The mystery was nicely executed, with bits and pieces of clues here and there as well as humorous interludes that enhanced the telling of this tale. This is another great addition to this engagingly entertaining series and I'm patiently waiting for the wedding of the century." – Dru's Book Musings

Books by Lois Winston

Anastasia Pollack Crafting Mystery series
Assault with a Deadly Glue Gun
Death by Killer Mop Doll
Revenge of the Crafty Corpse
Decoupage Can Be Deadly
A Stitch to Die For
Scrapbook of Murder
Drop Dead Ornaments
Handmade Ho-Ho Homicide
A Sew Deadly Cruise
Stitch, Bake, Die!

Anastasia Pollack Crafting Mini-Mysteries
Crewel Intentions
Mosaic Mayhem
Patchwork Peril
Crafty Crimes (all 3 novellas in one volume)

Empty Nest Mystery Series
Definitely Dead
Literally Dead

Romantic Suspense
Love, Lies and a Double Shot of Deception
Lost in Manhattan (writing as Emma Carlyle)
Someone to Watch Over Me (writing as Emma Carlyle)

Romance and Chick Lit
Talk Gertie to Me
Four Uncles and a Wedding (writing as Emma Carlyle)
Hooking Mr. Right (writing as Emma Carlyle)
Finding Hope (Writing as Emma Carlyle)

Novellas and Novelettes
Elementary, My Dear Gertie
Moms in Black, A Mom Squad Caper
Once Upon a Romance
Finding Mr. Right

Children's Chapter Book
The Magic Paintbrush

Nonfiction
Top Ten Reasons Your Novel is Rejected
House Unauthorized
Bake, Love, Write
We'd Rather Be Writing

Scrapbook
of Murder

LOIS WINSTON

Cover design by L. Winston

ISBN:978-1-940795-42-3

DEDICATION

In memory of Carolyn Grayson

ACKNOWLEDGMENTS

Special thanks to Donnell Bell and Irene Peterson for their superb editorial skills.

ONE

"Lupe called me at work this afternoon," I told Zack. We had escaped after dinner to his apartment. Situated above my detached garage, it afforded us a spot out of earshot of my mother-in-law Lucille, whose contempt for Zack grew exponentially with each passing day. Being permanently saddled with the woman was hard enough on a good day. Today was not a good day.

Zack finished pouring two glasses of chardonnay and handed one to me. I wandered over to the sofa and curled up in the corner. He followed, taking a seat next to me. The seconds ticked by. He shifted his body to face me. I suppose he was waiting for me to say something further, but my brain had stopped sending signals to my mouth.

Zack continued to wait. And wait. And wait some more. Finally, he asked, "Should I run an errand during this extremely long, pregnant pause, or are you planning to elaborate sometime soon?"

I heaved a sigh, then polished off half my wine before

answering him. "She asked if she could come over this evening to talk."

"About?"

I speared him with my best *duh!* look. "Isn't it obvious?"

"You have to stop blaming yourself, Anastasia. You're not responsible for what happened."

Right. And the captain of the Titanic wasn't responsible for steering his ship into a giant iceberg. "Carmen is dead because of me. How can Lupe not blame me?"

Lupe Betancourt is Carmen Cordova's daughter. She grew up down the street from me. Years ago she occasionally babysat my boys. Now they often babysit her kids. Or they did. I doubt Lupe will want any of us Pollacks in her home ever again.

Two-and-a-half weeks ago Lawrence Tuttnauer, my mother's sixth and latest husband, was arrested for orchestrating the cold-blooded murders of two of my neighbors, Lupe's mother Carmen and Betty Bentworth. He'd never met either of them. His hit man had chosen them at random because Lawrence wanted my attention diverted from the suspicious death of his daughter Cynthia. I didn't know it at the time, but I'd poked my nose into the wrong person's business.

As it turned out, so had Cynthia, but she'd gone a step further and threatened her old man. So Lawrence did what any connected guy in New Jersey would do—he took out a contract on her. No Father of the Year Award for him.

Although I had no regrets over the role I'd played in bringing Lawrence Tuttnauer to justice, guilt consumed me regarding the deaths of Betty and Carmen—especially Carmen. Not that nasty Betty Bentworth deserved a bullet to the skull, but no one had shed any tears over her demise, unlike the neighborhood's reaction to Carmen's gruesome death days before Halloween.

It doesn't help that every time I look at Lupe, I see a younger, thinner version of her mother. She's a living reminder of my culpability in her mother's death.

Mama and Lawrence married a month ago after a whirlwind courtship. She said he owned a commercial laundry. Turns out his enterprise laundered greenbacks, not linens, and he serviced only one client—the mob.

My name is Anastasia Pollack, and less than a year ago I led the life of a typical suburban, middle-class working mom. That all changed the day my husband dropped dead in a Las Vegas casino. I thought he was at a sales meeting in Harrisburg, Pennsylvania. I also thought we were debt-free with a comfortable nest egg squirreled away.

Instead, I discovered Karl Marx Pollack, now dubbed Dead Louse of a Spouse, had carried on a long-standing affair with Lady Not-So-Lucky. Karl not only gambled away our savings and our teenage sons' college funds, he'd taken out a second mortgage on the house, failed to pay our taxes for the last few years, maxed out our credit cards, and allowed his life insurance policy to lapse.

Strapping me with debt equal to the gross national product of Uzbekistan wasn't the worst of his sins, though. Nor was the homicidal loan shark he'd stiffed for fifty thousand dollars who demanded I pay up—or else. No, Karl's worst sin was sticking me with a communist mother-in-law from Hades.

I stared into my half-empty wineglass, avoiding eye contact with Zack, and forced my brain out of stall-mode. "I asked Lupe to meet me here."

"In my apartment?"

"I hope you don't mind."

The apartment used to be my home office. Zack is an award-winning photojournalist. Possibly a spy. Probably both. Anyway, prior to moving above my garage, he lived in Manhattan. However, he'd suffered through one too many police raids due to suspicious neighbors claiming he was operating a meth lab in his darkroom. He was on the hunt for a quiet suburban location without shared walls; I was desperate for rent money. The apartment over my garage fulfilled both of our needs.

Less than a year ago we were complete strangers. Now we're much more—the one and only good thing to come out of Dead Louse of a Spouse's betrayal.

"Do you want me to stay, or should I go run that errand?" asked Zack.

"You really have an errand to run?"

"No, but I'm sure I can find something to do."

"Are you kidding? Don't you dare leave me alone. I need all the moral support I can get."

Zack wrapped an arm around my shoulders and drew me closer. "You've got me, but have you thought about what you're going to say to Lupe?"

Lupe and I hadn't spoken since Carmen's funeral, which occurred days before I connected the dots leading to Lawrence's arrest. Once that line intersected directly through me, I morphed into a yellow-bellied coward. I didn't exactly go out of my way to avoid Lupe, but I hadn't reached out to her, either. "Like what? *So sorry I got nosy, and to throw me off, my mother's psychotic husband paid a homicidal maniac to kill your mother?* What are the odds of that conversation ending well?"

"Slim to none."

"Exactly."

"Maybe the best thing to do is accept whatever verbal tirade she hurls at you. She has a right to be angry."

"Of course, she does." If our roles were reversed, and Lupe had caused Mama's death, I'd want to throttle her. "But what if she wants to do more than scream at me?"

"Are you worried she'll turn violent?"

"I'm more worried she might file a wrongful death lawsuit. She could, couldn't she?"

Zack shrugged. "I'm not a lawyer."

"Neither am I, but even if a judge tossed the suit out of court, I'd still have to hire an attorney." I was barely making ends meet as it was. Paying down the Mount Everest of debt Karl had saddled me with took every discretionary penny I could claw out of my meager weekly budget. Damn him! After nearly a year, even with taking on a variety of moonlighting jobs, I'd only made little more than a miniscule dent, thanks to the devil known as compound interest. I couldn't afford to add legal fees to my teetering tower of monthly bills.

"This is all Karl's fault," I said.

Zack raised an eyebrow. "How so?"

"Don't you think it's a bit too coincidental that murder victims started showing up in my life shortly after Karl dropped dead? I've morphed into the Jessica Fletcher of Westfield, New Jersey."

Zack attempted to cover up a chortle with a forced cough. He failed miserably. "A bit of a stretch, not to mention a whopper of a rationalization."

"Is it?" I heaved a sigh and shrugged. "How about when all else fails, blame someone else?" Not that doing so made me feel any less guilty over Carmen's—and Betty's—deaths.

5

Our conversation halted at the sound of footsteps on the staircase leading up to the apartment. As Zack rose to answer the door, my pulsed raced. He opened the door at the first knock and said, "Come in, Lupe."

I rose from the sofa as Lupe stepped into the living room. She hugged a large, worn suitcase to her chest. Her eyes darted around the room. When they landed on me, she said, "Thanks for seeing me, Anastasia."

Normally I'd utter something like *my pleasure* or *no problem*, but in this case I anticipated a lack of pleasure and a multitude of problems. Still, not wanting to appear defensive, I forced a smile even if appropriate words failed me.

Zack came to my rescue. "Have a seat, Lupe. Would you like a glass of wine?"

She hesitated for a moment before settling into a chair opposite the sofa. As I resumed my seat, Lupe placed the suitcase on the floor beside her chair and said, "I'd love a glass. Thank you." Then she heaved a shuddering sigh, not the body language I'd expect from someone with an antagonistic agenda.

I glanced at the beat-up suitcase, classic striped tweed from the nineteen-forties or earlier. The leather trim and handles were gouged and scuffed, the brass hardware pitted and aged to near black. Even though I'd never been on the receiving end of a lawsuit, I was fairly certain they arrived in thin envelopes from process servers, not in vintage suitcases from the wronged party.

For the briefest of moments another thought flitted through my brain. I gave myself a mental slap to dispel the unwelcome wave of paranoia. If Lupe wanted me dead, she wouldn't blow herself up in the process. Besides, I sensed no evil vibe radiating from her, no invisible poisonous daggers shooting toward me.

The light had gone out of Lupe's once-luminous dark eyes. Her hair, normally lustrous ebony waves that bounced upon her shoulders, hung flat and limp against her head. Her face showed only sadness, certainly understandable considering she'd recently lost her mother to a violent crime. But a crime she could justifiably lay at my feet.

I should learn to mind my own business. Yet how could I have known the lengths Lawrence would go to protect his secrets? Ignoring the red flags may very well have put my family in danger. After all, the man had married my mother. If he was willing to kill his own daughter, how safe were the rest of us?

As heartbroken and guilt-ridden as I was that Carmen had paid the ultimate price just for living down the street from me, my actions may have saved countless other lives. Cold comfort but it was all I had at the moment.

Zack returned with a glass of wine for Lupe, along with the open wine bottle. He refilled my glass and topped off his before joining me on the sofa. "How are you holding up?" he asked Lupe.

She took a sip of wine before saying, "I think I'm still too numb to process my emotions."

I knew I had to shake off that proverbial cat that had snatched my tongue. My silence had grown awkward. I took a swig of chardonnay for fortification, then asked, "Is there anything we can do to help you?"

Lupe glanced down at the suitcase. "Actually, that's why I'm here. I've been sorting through Mami's possessions, getting the house ready to sell."

"That must be hard for you," I said, knowing Carmen's murder occurred in her home.

"Extremely." Her eyes filled with tears. "All the love that filled that house, all those memories, they're now forever tainted by such horrific evil. I can't wrap my head around it. So for now I push it aside and keep busy sorting through everything, deciding what to keep, what to toss, what to donate. The day I walk out of that house for the last time will be the day I give myself permission to start dealing with my grief and hopefully begin healing."

I inhaled a ragged breath. "You shouldn't have to take care of the house on your own, Lupe."

"Strangely enough, the busywork and minutia keep me from dwelling on the murder. I suppose I'm still in the denial phase. I have had help, though, from my husband, my aunt and a few other relatives."

She hoisted the suitcase off the floor and placed it on the coffee table between us. "I can handle sorting through kitchen cabinets and bookcases, even going through Mami's clothing and jewelry, but I came across something I can't handle. Not now. Maybe not ever. That's why I'm here, to ask a huge favor."

A huge favor? No accusations? No lawsuit? I could do a favor, the huger the better. Heck, I'd do a dozen huge favors for Lupe. A score. A hundred, even. Whatever it took. Not that any amount of favors would ever eradicate the guilt I felt over Carmen's death.

"I found this suitcase up in the attic." Lupe leaned forward, released the latches, and opened the lid. The suitcase was brimming with yellowed newspaper clippings, tattered envelopes, and old black-and-white photographs, some square, some rectangular, all with white deckled edges.

"From what I can tell," said Lupe, "these are family photos and assorted papers from before Mami and her family fled Cuba after the revolution. Mami led me to believe they left with nothing more than the clothes on their backs. I had no idea any of this existed."

"Have you gone through the contents?" I asked.

Lupe shook her head. "I couldn't bring myself to do more than glance at a few of the snapshots on top."

Zack picked up a photo of a young couple, both dressed in crisp white linen, the man in a suit, the woman in a sundress. They stood under a palm tree against a background of ocean waves lapping a sandy shore. He flipped the photo over and read the inscription. "*Maria y Miguel Ortiz, 1947.*"

"My mother's parents," said Lupe.

"What is it you want me to do?" I asked.

Lupe inhaled a deep breath, releasing it in a rush. "I know it's asking a lot, Anastasia, but I'd be so grateful if you'd organize all of this into a scrapbook for my children. It would provide them a connection to their Cuban heritage."

I stared into the suitcase, admittedly overwhelmed by the prospect of making sense of the contents. Where did I even begin? "How? I have no idea who any of these people are."

"I'm hoping most of the photos are labeled. The ones I looked at were." She rooted in her purse, pulled out a folded sheet of paper, and handed it to me. "My aunt created a family tree a few years ago. I made a copy for you."

I perused the ancestral genealogy, which went back generations prior to the invention of photography. According to what I could decipher with my rusty high school Spanish, Lupe's relatives originally hailed from northern Spain and arrived in Cuba in the late eighteenth century. I'd only have to deal with the family members whose images filled the suitcase. Still, the task was daunting and would take weeks, if not months, given my limited free time.

I glanced up at Lupe. She sat on the edge of her chair, worrying her lower lip as she awaited my answer. How could I say no? Hadn't I just told myself no favor would be too huge an imposition, given the amount of guilt I carried with me?

"You realize this isn't something I can accomplish in a few days," I said.

"Take as much time as you need. And I'm more than happy to pay you, Anastasia." She paused for a moment before adding, "Rumor has it you've had some financial setbacks since Karl died."

My jaw dropped. I'd worked hard to keep my neighbors from finding out about the mess Dead Louse of a Spouse had dumped on me. "How did you—?"

"Your mother told Mami what happened."

Thank you, Mama! How many other people had she blabbed to about my indebtedness? Heck, she probably took out a full-page ad in the *Westfield Leader*, which I never would have known because I'd cancelled my subscription as one of my many cost-cutting measures.

As if reading my mind, Zack squeezed my hand. I'd deal with Mama later. She's just lucky she's no longer living with me or there would be fireworks at Casa Pollack tonight.

"Will you do it?" asked Lupe.

"There are people who specialize in this sort of thing," I said.

Lupe shook her head. "I can't trust total strangers with this. They didn't know Mami. To them this would be just another job. You were my mother's friend. I trust you, Anastasia, and with your crafts background, I know you'll create something beautiful that my children will treasure."

I carefully leafed through some of the papers and photos in the suitcase, taking care to avoid touching the newspaper clippings.

They looked so brittle I feared they'd disintegrate in my hands. Many of the photos weren't in much better condition. Few people had knowledge of archival preservation back when one of Lupe's relatives dumped all of these memories into a suitcase. Time and the chemical composition of the suitcase interior had faded and yellowed the photos. Many bore brown spots from residual fingerprints. Being stored in a non-climate-controlled attic for decades had added insult to injury.

Lupe sat on the edge of her chair, her eyes pleading, as she waited for my answer.

"Of course, but given the fragile nature of most of these items, I'm not sure how long a scrapbook would last." I gently picked up a church program from Carmen's first communion. As careful as I was, a corner flaked off in my hand. "See what I mean?"

She nodded.

Zack peered into the suitcase and sighed. "Anastasia is right. Unfortunately, most of the originals won't last much longer. Another few years in the attic, and you probably would have opened the suitcase to find a pile of confetti."

"Is there anything you can do?" asked Lupe.

"We could scan the originals to create printed photo albums," said Zack. "That way we could also remove some of the discoloration."

We? I turned to him. "You'd be willing to help?"

"If I don't, I won't see you for several months."

"You two are the best," said Lupe. A tear slid down her cheek. "I can't begin to tell you how much this means to me."

"Anything for you, Lupe," said Zack, but when he squeezed my knee again, I knew his offer was more about me than Lupe. The God of Second Chances had certainly smiled down on me the day

Zachary Barnes decided to rent the apartment above my garage.

~*~

The next day genius struck as I sat in morning rush hour traffic on my way to work. If I incorporated Lupe's scrapbook into a magazine spread, I'd be able to spend time on the project during office hours and kill the proverbial two birds with one stone—or in this case, two craft projects with one scrapbook.

As the crafts editor for *American Woman*, a third-rate monthly magazine sold primarily at supermarket checkout counters, I was tasked with developing themes and projects that wouldn't intimidate our readership. Quick and easy reigned throughout the pages of each issue of our magazine.

A week remained before our monthly staff meeting where our editors planned the issue five months down the road, as well as provided status updates on the various other issues in the works. I'd already put together my presentation, but I could easily save that idea for the following month, substituting a feature on scrapbooking crafts for the upcoming issue. What better way to commemorate all the graduations and weddings that fill the spring calendar than to create lasting memories of them? Why hadn't I thought of that earlier?

Since such brilliance definitely warranted a reward, once I arrived at work, I detoured toward the break room before heading to my cubicle. One of the perks of working at *American Woman* is a never-ending supply of yummy edibles from companies hoping for endorsements from Cloris McWerther, our food editor, who graciously shares her bounty with the rest of us. We're also the beneficiaries of the delicacies she whips up in our test kitchen.

Cloris isn't the only editor who receives swag from vendors. Manufacturers constantly send me their latest products, eager to see them featured in craft projects in our magazine. However, unlike cookies, cupcakes, and croissants, you can't eat pompoms, felt squares, and glitter paint. On the upside, pompoms, felt squares, and glitter paint contain no calories. Between Cloris, my lack of willpower, and my aversion to any form of exercise, after seventeen years, I've given up hope of ever shedding my post-maternity pounds.

I'd probably hate Cloris if she weren't my best friend. She's a Size Two with a metabolism that treats calories like water, flushing them from her system before they ever have a chance to attach to her stomach, hips, or thighs. I, on the other hand, only have to breathe in the aroma of freshly baked chocolate chip cookies to add five pounds, ten if I actually take a bite.

Pushing all thoughts of weight loss aside, I entered the break room to find that the pastry gods were smiling down on me this morning. A large platter of meringue-topped, mystery tartlets sat next to the coffee pot. With the meringue covering the entire top of the tart, I had no idea what lay beneath, but I didn't care. Cloris never failed to provide out-of-this-world delights. I grabbed a paper plate and helped myself to two tartlets before my fellow editors and the support staff discovered them. After pouring a cup of coffee, I continued on to my cubicle.

"You make these?" I asked Cloris, stopping at the entrance to her cubicle, located directly across from mine, and pointing to the goodies on my plate.

She nodded. "You're all my guinea pigs today. If everyone likes them, they go on my Thanksgiving menu."

I groaned.

Cloris's eyes widened, her eyebrows arching up toward the gingerbread-colored wispy bangs of her pixie haircut. "What's wrong? You haven't even taken a bite."

"I'm sure they're scrumptious. It's the mention of Thanksgiving. I keep putting off thinking about it."

"You can't put it off much longer. It's only three days away."

I groaned again. "Don't remind me."

"Are you cooking?"

"Ira invited all of us to his place." Ira Pollack was my deceased husband's long-lost half-brother. He'd been married to trophy wife Cynthia before her father had her whacked. Look up *needy* in Webster's, and you'll find a picture of Ira. He's been wheedling his way into our lives ever since he discovered our existence last summer. Unfortunately, he's got the money to buy whatever he thinks will accomplish this.

I've tried declining his generosity, but I'm often guilt-tripped into accepting, either by Ira himself, my mother, or my sons. He's currently trying to make up for introducing Mama to Lawrence—not to mention for Lawrence nearly killing us.

"Ira's cooking?"

"I doubt he knows how to boil water. I'm assuming he's having the dinner catered."

Cloris wagged her finger at me. "You need to learn to say no."

I shrugged. "I tried, but part of me feels sorry for him. He's like a lost puppy."

"And you're a softie."

"Maybe, but he'd only invite himself and his spoiled brats over to my house if I declined his invitation." Ira's first wife died of cancer, leaving him with three hellions who are experts in the art of wrapping their father around their pinkies.

Cloris shook her head. "*No* is usually one of the first words kids learn. You must have skipped the terrible twos."

"I doubt Mama would agree with you. Anyway, at least at Ira's house I won't have to listen to his kids whine about Casa Pollack's lack of amenities."

"What's wrong with your house? Last time I looked, you had indoor plumbing."

"But no flat-screen TV, which places us squarely in the Dark Ages."

"It's a wonder you survive." Cloris pointed to the pastry in my hand. "Eat a tart. You'll feel better."

I placed my coffee cup on the edge of her desk, lifted one of the tarts off the paper plate, and devoured half of it in one bite. Pumpkin, cranberry, pecan, and meringue exploded on my taste buds, creating a full-blown gastronomic orgasm in my mouth.

Cloris had created a shell made of brown sugar, butter, and crushed pecans. On top of the crust she'd spread a thin layer of cranberry compote, then filled the tart with lighter-than-air whipped pumpkin custard drizzled with more cranberry. She'd topped that with a perfectly flamed meringue. A bite later I'd devoured the entire tart without coming up for air.

"That was incredible," I said, licking my fingers. "How could anyone not love these?"

She grinned. "Just had to be sure."

I eyed the second tart. Before devouring it, I said, "Your false modesty would be extremely annoying if you weren't such a fabulous baker."

Before Cloris could mouth a comeback, her office phone rang. "I'll let you get to that," I said, grabbing my coffee cup and scooting across the hall.

As I settled into my desk chair I heard her say, "That's odd. I'll be right down."

Five minutes later she returned, but instead of going into her cubicle, she stormed into mine. Wildly waving a fistful of papers in the air, she screamed, "I don't believe this!"

TWO

I immediately rose to my feet. Very little ever flapped the unflappable Cloris and never into the manic frenzy I now witnessed. Seeing her doing a spot-on imitation of a purple-faced cartoon character, complete with an erupting head, scared the crap out of me. I thought she'd stroke out any minute. I reached for her arm and forced her into the extra chair in my cubicle. "Calm down."

"Calm down?" Her voice climbed several octaves. "Not likely."

I debated leaving her to grab a bottle of water from the break room but quickly decided against it. Having nothing else to offer her, I yanked the papers from her fist and forced the remainder of my coffee into her hands. "Fine. Don't calm down. Drink this. Then tell me what's going on." Hopefully the caffeine wouldn't contribute to her already stroke-inducing state.

Cloris took a few sips, followed by several deep breaths. As her complexion faded from apoplectic to several shades above nearly normal, my urge to call 911 abated.

"Well?" I asked after my non-medical expertise assured me she no longer stood on the precipice of death.

"We're being sued," she said.

"The magazine?" This made no sense. Why would the food editor receive this information before the cadre of corporate suits with their high-priced law degrees hanging on the walls of their corner offices? Unless... "Is someone claiming one of your recipes poisoned her?"

Cloris's eyes widened. "What! Of course not! Why would you say such a thing?"

"But you just said the magazine is being sued."

"Not the magazine. Me. And Gregg."

I held up my hand. "Stop. Don't say another word."

I stepped out of my cubicle and scanned left and right, making certain no one was within earshot. Then I checked the cubicles to either side of Cloris's and mine. All empty.

Still, no sense taking any chances. I grabbed Cloris's arm and led her down the corridor to the conference room. Once inside, I closed and locked the door. "Okay," I said. "Start from the beginning. Who's suing you and why?"

"The people who bought our home. They claim the house has a stalker, that Gregg and I knew about it, and we deliberately withheld the information in our disclosure documents."

"That's absurd. You can't stalk a house. It sits there on its foundation and never moves." I'm intimately familiar with the stalker M.O., having recently dealt with my own stalker. Stalkers don't stalk houses; they stalk people. Besides, if someone had at any time lurked around Cloris's property, she would have called the police.

"Why now? You sold your house six months ago." Cloris and

Gregg had downsized to a townhouse in Springfield as a way to pay for their daughter's college education.

"They were renovating the house—doing what, I can't imagine."

Neither could I. Cloris had owned a comfortable shabby chic Victorian that needed no updating, let alone a massive renovation. If any house needed renovating, it was my shabby, far from chic mid-century rancher.

"Anyway," she continued, "they haven't moved in yet. Now they're saying they can't because they've received threatening letters from some deranged psycho who's claiming ownership of the house."

"How does that have anything to do with you?"

Cloris drained the remains of the coffee and tossed the cup in the trash. "According to the lawsuit, we received a letter several days before closing and didn't tell them about it."

"Did you?"

"Of course not!"

"Then what proof do they have that you received a letter?"

"The psycho claims to have been in communication with us."

"Well, that's certainly credible evidence."

"It gets better. Look here." She pulled the papers from my hand and stabbed at a paragraph. "According to this, they received the first of several letters three days after taking possession of the house."

"Yet they still went ahead with renovations and waited six months to file the lawsuit? Sounds to me like a case of buyer's remorse. They're looking for a way to make you and Gregg pay for their mistake."

"Not only us. They're also suing our realtor, the title insurance company, and the escrow settlement company. And you know the worst part of all this?"

"What?"

Cloris dropped down into one of the chairs surrounding the conference table and lowered her head into her hands. "Defending this lawsuit could cost us all the profit we made on the sale of the house. Or more. We might as well not have downsized."

Exactly my thoughts, but instead of agreeing and making Cloris feel even worse, I tried to downplay her fears. "Hopefully that won't be the case. I can't imagine any sensible judge not tossing this out as a meritless nuisance suit. For all you know, they wrote those letters themselves."

"Let's hope you're right. My daughter's college education hangs in the balance."

"Have you spoken with Gregg yet? He must have also been served with papers."

Cloris heaved herself from the chair as if she carried around a couple of hundred extra pounds on her ultra-thin frame. "He's flying back from a business trip. For all I know, a process server will be waiting for him at the airport."

"You need to call a lawyer. I don't think you can use the one you used for the closing if he's named in the suit."

"I know. Today's to-do list is getting longer by the minute."

"Let me know if I can do anything to help."

Cloris brightened. "Got a magic wand?"

If I did, I would have used it long ago to improve my financial situation. "Sorry, but if I find one, you'll be the first to know."

Cloris shrugged. "Moving on to Plan B, then."

"Plan B?"

"You summon your inner Miss Marple to dig up some mud on

these litigious lowlifes."

That wasn't the kind of help I had in mind, but ever since I began stumbling across dead bodies, everyone assumes I have some kind of crime-solving super power. In reality, my snooping has nearly gotten me killed on several occasions. My luck could run out at any moment. Besides, I had my kids to consider. They'd already lost their father this past year. I couldn't get myself killed and abandon them to the care of their grandmothers. They'd kill me—except that I'd already be dead.

However, given that Cloris saved my life several months ago, I owed her big time, and thankfully, there were no dead bodies involved in her plight. I just wasn't sure what I could do to help her with a lawsuit. Still, I felt obligated to try. "Get me whatever information you can, and I'll see what I can do. Zack might have some ideas. Or maybe he can pick Patricia's brain."

Patricia was Zack's ex-wife and an assistant district attorney in New York. They had the friendliest divorce on the planet. Her twins from her second marriage even called him Uncle Zacky.

"That's the best news I've heard all day."

I offered Cloris my best Pollyanna smile. "The day is young. You might hear some more before it's over."

"The way my luck is going?"

"Hey, I'm the one with the rotten luck. Your husband didn't die and leave you one step from calling a cardboard box home."

"No offense, but right now I'm beginning to think that rotten luck of yours is contagious. We might need to negotiate a two-for-one deal on inhabitable cardboard boxes."

I certainly hoped not. I unlocked the conference room door, and we both returned to our cubicles. A few minutes later from across the hall I heard Cloris placing a call to her attorney. I jumped out of my chair and dashed across the short distance that separated our two cubicles. "What are you doing?"

Her brows knit together in consternation as she cupped her hand over the phone's speaker. "Calling the attorney who handled our house sale to ask him for recommendations of other lawyers."

I rolled my eyes at her. "Why do you think I stopped you earlier and dragged you into the conference room? You don't want anyone overhearing your conversation."

She slapped her forehead as she popped out of her chair. "See what this lawsuit has done to me? What would I do without you?" she asked as she scurried back down the hall.

I returned to my cubicle and fired up my computer. Time to rewrite my proposal in order to kill those two birds with one scrapbooking project.

~*~

I arrived home from work to find my mother-in-law and her commie cohorts, the twelve other octogenarian members of the Daughters of the October Revolution, had once again taken over my home to plan one of their protests. Judging from the dirty cups, glasses, and dishes scattered around my living and dining room, they'd also raided the refrigerator and pantry.

Harriet Kleinhample, a woman whose oversized attitude made up for her diminutive stature, shot me her trademark evil eye and demanded, "What happened to your printer?"

Several months ago I arrived home to find my computer printer plugged into her laptop and spewing forth page after page of full-color, high quality flyers that were quickly drinking up my last color ink cartridges. They'd also helped themselves to a ream of my paper. I learned my lesson. All of my supplies are now locked away in Zack's apartment. Maybe I also needed to padlock my fridge and pantry.

"Looks like you have a printer," I said, nodding at the one presently churning out more communist manifestos for their cause du jour.

"We had to buy one, thanks to your selfishness," said Lucille. "I should deduct the cost from the rent I pay you. We're all on fixed incomes, you know."

And I'm not? My mother-in-law lives in her own reality. When I requested she kick in a nominal amount of money for her room and board after Karl left me in debt up the wazoo, she labeled me a slumlord.

What she didn't know was that her precious Karl had plotted to kill her so he could abscond with the life savings she kept in shoeboxes under her bed. Although she survived, she was now penniless except for her monthly social security check and a miniscule pension. Tempted as I am to tell her the truth about her son, it would be an exercise in futility. She'd only accuse me, yet again, of besmirching his good name.

In no mood for a war of words with thirteen nasty old commies, I ignored Harriet, Lucille, and the rest of their gang and marched into the kitchen where I found the caked-on remnants of the lasagna I'd planned to serve for dinner sitting on the kitchen table. It's a good thing my blood pressure normally runs on the low side. Otherwise, I might have blown a gasket at that moment. Instead, I stormed out the back door into the windswept, raw night and stomped across the semi-frozen yard to the garage. Zack opened the door and stepped out onto the landing before I'd climbed halfway up the staircase.

I opened my mouth to speak, but before I could utter a word, he said, "I know," and handed me a glass of pinot noir. "The boys arrived home about fifteen minutes ago and told me," he continued as I entered the apartment. "I sent them out to pick up some dinner for us."

"My life sucks," I complained, sinking into the sofa cushions.

He raised an eyebrow. "All of it?"

I sighed. "All except for you and the boys. And maybe Mama, but the jury's still out on her lately."

I polished off the remnants of my wine as I glanced around the apartment that less than a year ago had housed my home studio. Silently, I offered up a prayer of thanks to the God of Financially Strapped Widows. He could have sent me a couple of rowdy college students or a divorcee with several kids as tenants. Instead, he'd decided my bleak life needed a bit of eye candy and blessed me with a man whose genes spent time cavorting in the same primordial soup as Pierce Brosnan, George Clooney, Patrick Dempsey, and Antonio Banderas.

At first I tamped down my traitorous hormones. After all, what could a guy like Zack possibly see in me, a Bartlett-shaped mom with enough baggage to fill a tramp steamer? A lot, as it turns out. Not only did Zack Barnes upend every single one of my preconceptions, I'm convinced I never would have survived the past year without him.

Case in point, the collapsible metal table set up in the far corner of the room. Zack often used the table as a supplemental workstation when sorting through large numbers of prints from a photographic assignment. I rose from the sofa, crossed the room, and studied the table's contents. A white sheet covered the table. On the far left Zack had created three neat stacks of snapshots, next to which he'd spread out a dozen more. The second half of the table contained yellowing newspaper clippings that he'd sandwiched between sheets of clear plastic. "You started without me?"

He shrugged. "I'm between assignments. I've got the time right now. You hardly have a moment to breathe during the week."

Not that I had more than a few moments on any given weekend, either, thanks to the joys of single parenthood. At least Alex was now driving, which allowed for a divide-and-conquer approach to weekend errands.

I wrapped my arms around Zack's neck and asked, "Did anyone ever tell you you're too good to be true?" I then rewarded him with a kiss that promised more to come.

"Don't get too excited," he said. "I only scanned about a quarter of the photos so far."

"And these?" I asked pointing to the newspaper clippings.

"Not scanned yet. Merely temporarily preserved. I couldn't run the risk of moving them more than once. The plastic will keep them from disintegrating when we handle them. Once everything is scanned, we can sort through the images and articles to decide which ones to digitally restore for the scrapbook."

I frowned at the clippings. "How good is your Spanish, really? I got the feeling Lupe might never be in the right frame of mind to translate any of this."

"I'm fully fluent."

I raised an eyebrow. "From all those alphabet agency assignments?"

"From all those *photographic* assignments."

I smirked. "Of course."

"You're never going to believe me, are you?"

"Methinks the gentleman doth protest too much. I'll believe you when you tell me the truth." I was convinced Zack's photojournalism was a cover for his real job as a government operative.

"You have an overactive imagination."

"So you've said." On more than one occasion. I still didn't believe him and probably never would. The man owned a badass gun, and he knew how to use it. Not that owning a gun made him a spy. However, combined with his frequent secretive trips and all the people he knew who had all sorts of information at their fingertips, even a math-challenged crafts editor could put two and two together and come up with SPY.

Still, a part of me hoped Zack was right about my overactive imagination. I'd experienced too many encounters with the seamier side of society over the past year. Far too often I'd spent the night tossing and turning, unable to sleep from fear for my own safety and that of my kids. I didn't need to add Zack into the mix. As it was, every time he left on a photo assignment, I conjured up all sorts of lurid images of him stepping into traps set by smugglers, gangbangers, or terrorists. I'm not sure I could deal with knowing those possibilities were far more real than imaginary.

In any case, at that moment all conversation regarding Zack's true profession came to a halt with the sound of footsteps on the outside staircase leading up to the apartment. A moment later the door flew open, heralding the arrival of Alex and Nick, along with the aromas of Moo Shu Shrimp, fried rice, spareribs, and spring rolls.

Throughout dinner I noticed Alex and Nick exchanging silent communications. At first, I dismissed it. My teenage sons are certainly allowed conversations that don't involve parent participation. However, these generally don't occur literally under my nose. After the third semi-surreptitious sideways glance at each other, I called them on it, "What's going on with you two?"

"You tell her," said Alex.

"You're older," said Nick.

"Out with it," I said.

Alex inhaled a deep breath. I'd never seen my seventeen-year-old so nervous. I tamped down the panic building inside me and silently fired off a plea to the heavens that he hadn't gotten some girl pregnant. Karl had assured me he'd had "the talk" with both boys the moment they'd entered puberty as well as countless times since. But since Karl had lied about so many things, after his death I broached the subject with Alex and Nick. The last thing a teenage boy wants is to talk to his mother about sex, but both my sons made it clear they weren't about to screw up their lives. They told me not to worry. But isn't that what all teenagers tell their mothers?

No, I quickly assured myself. It's got to be something else, something not as life shattering as a teen pregnancy, given that Alex had urged Nick to take on the role of spokesman. Panic returned as I stared into the blue-gray eyes of my youngest son. Nick might be fifteen, but he was still my baby. Surely, he hadn't—

"We refuse to go to Uncle Ira's for Thanksgiving," said Alex.

My relief burst forth in an uproarious belly laugh. There have been times when my sons have looked at me as if I had two heads, both covered in pink and purple polka dots. This was one of those times.

I waved away their looks of concern and surprised them by saying, "I don't want to go, either."

"Then why are we going?" asked Nick.

"Sometimes gifts come with strings attached. Ira has been very good to you...to us. We owe it to him to show up."

"So we have to do what he wants from now until forever?" asked Alex.

"He's a lonely man who's been through a lot," I said. Within the span of a few years Ira had lost both his parents and his wife to illnesses. Then he discovered he had a long-lost half-brother, only to find Karl had recently died. A few months later, a murder orchestrated by Ira's father-in-law claimed his second wife. Was it any wonder the guy was so needy that he tripped over himself trying to buy his way into our lives?

"Maybe it's time we had a short respite from Ira," said Zack.

"How about permanent?" asked Nick.

I speared him with my mom look before asking Zack, "How do we do that without hurting his feelings?"

"His feelings?" asked Nick. "What about our feelings? We're the ones who have to put up with his spoiled brats."

"Uncle Ira wouldn't be half-bad without Melody, Harmony, and Isaac," said Alex.

"Unfortunately, they're a package deal," I said.

"I think it's time for some tough love," said Zack. He pulled his phone from his pocket.

"What are you doing?" I asked.

"Temporarily relieving some of the stress in your life." Before I could say anything, Zack tapped his screen a few times, placed the phone to his ear and after a short pause said, "Hello, Ira. This is Zack Barnes...Fine...Listen, I'm sorry to disappoint you, but Anastasia, her mother, the boys, and I won't be able to make it for Thanksgiving...No, no one is ill...No, you can't bring Thanksgiving dinner here. We won't be home...It's a personal matter. We'll be in touch after the holiday...I'll tell her." With that he hung up the phone.

"I don't believe you just did that," I said, but at the same time I realized Zack's proactive actions had lifted a huge weight from my chest.

He winked at me. "Someone had to."

"What did he ask you to tell me?"

"He said if there's anything he can do to help, you shouldn't hesitate to call him."

"He can help by not constantly butting into our lives," said Nick.

"So, what are we going to do for Thanksgiving?" asked Alex.

"We're dining out," said Zack. He placed another call and made dinner reservations for six at one of our favorite Westfield restaurants. To my amazement, they actually had a table available for Thursday evening.

"Six?" asked Alex when Zack disconnected from the call.

"It wouldn't be right to leave Lucille to fend for herself on Thanksgiving," said Zack.

"Why not?" asked Nick.

'Nick!" I glared at my son.

"She hates us," he said. "Why can't she spend Thanksgiving with those nasty old commie friends of hers?"

"Maybe she will, but we still have to extend an invitation," I said. "Remember, she does live here."

"Kind of hard to forget," said Nick.

THREE

After dinner the boys excused themselves to tackle their homework while Zack and I headed into the house to wrestle the mess Lucille and her minions had left before taking off to foment revolution somewhere—or watch *Dancing with the Stars* on Harriet Kleinhample's sixty-inch flat screen TV.

Who knew octogenarian commies had a thing for B-list celebrities and former politicians prancing around in sequins and stilettos?

Of course, Lucille hadn't bothered to take Devil Dog with her, which meant one of us would have to walk him at some point if I didn't want to wake up tomorrow morning to find doggie pee or worse soaked into my carpets.

The pooch in question was a lazy, lumbering French bulldog, much like his owner, minus the French connection. I would have thought a Russian wolfhound more in keeping with Lucille's political leanings, but maybe the breed was associated too closely with Russian nobility. I knew little about the preferred pets of the czars and even less about Russian wolfhounds in general.

Or Lucille's choice in dog may have had nothing to do with politics and everything to do with the minimal square footage of her former apartment. Since our conversations never progressed beyond her grievance du jour, I'd probably never know the reason for her choice of dog breed. Truthfully, I didn't care.

Lucille had named her precious pooch Manifesto, after the communist treatise of the same name. I can't imagine anyone, with the possible exception of Vladimir Putin, giving a pet such a name. Anyway, the dog had made it crystal-clear that he didn't want to live in my home any more than I wanted him here. So much to my mother-in-law's displeasure, I'd taken to referring to him as Mephisto the Devil Dog.

However, last summer Mephisto and I formed a détente of sorts. He even had a hand in saving my life, and now he prefers my company to Lucille's s'mothering. This definitely does not sit well with my mother-in-law. She's taken to punishing us both by taking off without notice for hours at a time, leaving me with one more household responsibility.

Mephisto was currently slurping water over my kitchen linoleum in a semi-futile attempt to transfer the liquid from his bowl to his mouth while maintaining a fixed gaze on Ralph, who surveyed the activity from his favorite perch atop my refrigerator. I'd inherited Ralph, an African Grey parrot, several years ago from my Great-aunt Penelope. At the time I would have preferred her collection of Royal Doulton china, but the talented bird has since grown on me, and unlike Mephisto, he's completely toilet trained and grooms himself.

"Heaven forbid those women bother to bring their dirty dishes into the kitchen, let alone load the dishwasher," I said as I deposited dried lasagna-encrusted plates and utensils on the counter. "So much for their communist work ethic. They act more like entitled nobility than the proletariat."

Zack stood at the sink, scraping food into the garbage disposer. "How was work today?" he asked.

I cocked my head and raised an eyebrow. "My, what a subtle segue."

"Face it. You're never going to change Lucille, so I might as well take a stab at changing the subject to reduce your blood pressure."

"First Ira, now Lucille, huh? Zachary Barnes: photojournalist, government operative, *and* shrink extraordinaire." I threw my arms up and laughed in spite of myself. "You win, Dr. Freud."

Why do I bother letting Lucille get under my epidermis? Best to take a more Zen-like approach to my mother-in-law. If I adjusted my attitude, I might even eliminate the acid reflux I'd developed shortly after she moved in with us.

So if Zack wanted to move the conversation in a different direction, I could accommodate. "Cloris and her husband are being sued by the people who bought their house."

He paused from his scraping and turned to look at me. "Seriously?"

"Unfortunately, yes."

"Why?"

I told him what I knew of the situation. When I'd finished my recap, I said, "Is it just me, or does something not sound quite Kosher in all this?"

"Forget non-Kosher. It sounds downright fraudulent."

"*The fraud of men was ever so, since summer first was leavy,*" squawked Ralph. "*Much Ado about Nothing.* Act Two, Scene Three."

Thanks to decades of sitting in on Great-Aunt Penelope's Shakespearean lectures, Ralph's tiny brain contained an encyclopedic knowledge of every play and sonnet ever written by the Bard. This had given him an uncanny talent for squawking situation-appropriate quotes.

Zack grabbed a chunk of tomato from the lasagna pan. After carefully inspecting it for any cheese, he rewarded Ralph with the morsel. Parrots are lactose intolerant, and along with doggie pee, I didn't need parrot poop all over my house.

"Did you have a chance to read the lawsuit?" asked Zack.

"Only the section that mentions the letters the buyers supposedly received."

"Did you know that when a lawsuit is filed, it becomes public record?"

As usual, Zack's brain overflowed with all sorts of knowledge that seemed unusual for a photojournalist—unless at some point in his past he'd sued someone or been sued. However, I decided to save that conversation for a future date. No point opening another can of fish bait this evening, given our earlier discussion regarding his spying duties. "Meaning?"

"We can probably find the lawsuit on the Internet."

After finishing the cleanup, I made Alex and Nick promise to walk Mephisto before they hunkered down to a post-homework evening of video games, then I returned with Zack to his apartment.

Within minutes we found a treasure trove of information about the lawsuit, thanks to the media already picking up the story. "Certainly didn't take them long," I said, scanning down the column of articles that had popped up in our Google search. Not only did we find the lawsuit posted in its entirety, within hours of the suit being filed, the story had gone global.

"Is it any wonder?" asked Zack as we read through the lawsuit. "This has the makings of a blockbuster horror movie. I'm betting the bidding war has already begun for the story rights."

According to the suit, the author of the letters, who called himself The Sentinel, claimed his family had kept watch over the house since it was first built in the nineteen twenties. He'd taken over the duties after his father's death two decades earlier. The Sentinel claimed he told Cloris and Gregg to move because now that their daughter had gone off to college, it was time to fill the house with fresh young blood, something the house needed to sustain itself while awaiting its second coming.

"The house's second coming? What does that mean?" I asked.

Zack shrugged. "Beats me. The guy is obviously nuts."

The lawsuit claimed the Sentinel went on to say in one of the three letters that both he and the house were extremely unhappy regarding the renovations done by the new owners. "How can a house be unhappy?" I asked.

"You can't look at this through a lens of logic," said Zack. "The guy is deranged. I can understand why the new owners refuse to move in. He's made overt threats to them and their children."

"He's also insinuating something is hidden in the walls and the attic. Wouldn't the contractors have uncovered whatever he's alluding to during the renovations?"

"I suppose it depends on the extent of the renovations. If they didn't open any walls, something could be hidden behind one of them."

"I was in the attic once. It's bare sheathing, studs, and rafters. Cloris and Gregg only used it to store their Christmas lawn ornaments. There's no place to hide anything."

We continued reading to the end of the lawsuit. "Interesting that the letters stopped after the third one," said Zack. Months had gone by without the new owners hearing further from The Sentinel. "Maybe he died or was arrested for another crime and is now in prison."

"Or maybe he never existed," I suggested. "What we haven't found in our Internet search are the actual letters posted anywhere online, only summaries and pull quotes. What if the new buyers are scam artists?"

"Another possibility. The police will investigate. I'm sure they'll check for fingerprints on the letters— "

"If there really are letters."

"If the new owners can't produce the letters, this becomes a fraud investigation."

"And if the letters exist?"

"The police will get writing samples from Cloris, Gregg, and the new owners."

"They're certainly not going to find Cloris or Gregg's fingerprints. Why would they send the letters? This is one huge headache for them, not to mention how much it's going to cost them to defend themselves."

"I know, but as absurd as it sounds, the police have to eliminate them as suspects."

I wondered if Zack's knowledge of police procedure stemmed from personal experience or from watching *Law & Order*. I filed that topic in the back of my brain for another day. "What can we do to help?"

Zack raised an eyebrow. "We?"

"Cloris is my closest friend. She saved my life. Literally. I have to do whatever I can to help her clear her name, and you've got all

36

sorts of professional contacts—"

He raised the other eyebrow. "Alphabet agency contacts?"

"I didn't say that, but since you brought it up..."

Zack huffed out a lungful of exasperation with a chuckle along for the ride. "As hard as you find it to believe, I don't have those sorts of contacts, but what I can do is see if Patricia has any suggestions for them."

I kissed the tip of his nose. "I'm sure Cloris would appreciate that."

"That's all I get?"

"Come to think of it, I do also owe you for rescuing us from Thanksgiving Hell."

"Damn straight." Zack pulled me into his arms and initiated a real kiss. I certainly didn't object. Afterwards he nodded in the direction of the apartment door. "Should I lock it?"

How I needed some real alone time with Zack! But as I was about to give in to temptation, out of the corner of my eye I caught a glimpse of the folding table covered in snapshots and newspaper clippings. Guilt immediately tossed an icy wet blanket over my raging hormones.

Zack followed the direction of my gaze and sighed. "Business before pleasure?"

I nodded.

He dropped his arms to his sides and sighed again. Then he stepped over to his desk and retrieved two pairs of white cotton gloves from a drawer. Handing one pair to me, he said, "You sort; I'll scan."

"Are these really necessary?" I asked as I donned the gloves.

"It's a precautionary measure. Any oils and acids from our skin will speed up the deterioration process, and this stuff is already in really bad shape."

We walked over to the folding table, and as Zack explained his system to me, he pointed from pile to pile. "These have already been scanned, these are the ones I separated out to scan but haven't gotten to yet, and these are photos we needn't bother with."

"Why not?"

"They're either out of focus, duplicates, or too far gone to use."

I pointed to the dozen photos spread out on the table. "And these?"

"The ones I was about to make decisions on when you arrived before dinner." He nodded in the direction of the suitcase. "There are probably several hundred more to go through when we're finished with these."

"Then we'd better get to work."

To a background score of classical jazz instrumentals, Zack and I worked for several hours, sorting and scanning the snapshots, newspaper clippings, and various other mementos of Carmen Cordova's Cuban heritage. The work was tedious, made that much worse by my poor Spanish skills and the struggle to decipher nearly undecipherable handwriting on the backs of many of the photos.

However, by eleven o'clock we'd managed to struggle our way through almost half the contents of the suitcase. I tried to stifle a yawn but failed miserably. Mr. Sandman beckoned.

"Time to call it a night?" asked Zack.

"Afraid so. My eyes are glazing over. Besides, one of us has to get up early tomorrow morning for work."

I reached for the suitcase lid, but as I began lowering it, I noticed a shifting of the fabric pocket stitched into the inside of the lid. The top edge of the pocket was gathered with elastic to keep any contents from falling out, but the elastic had rotted with age, and the pocket was no longer taut against the inside of the lid, causing the fabric to sag.

The movement I'd noticed wasn't simply a fluttering of loose fabric, though. The pocket held something that had shifted from the lowering of the lid. I raised the lid back up, slid my hand into the pocket, and removed a yellowing, sealed business envelope. I turned the envelope over, and much to my surprised, discovered it was addressed to Lupe.

"How odd," I said, more to myself than aloud.

"What?" asked Zack.

I held the envelope out toward him. "This appears to have been placed in the suitcase years ago, but it couldn't have come from Cuba with the other contents. It's addressed to Lupe."

"Lupe is a common Spanish name. It could be a relative."

"I suppose."

"There's one way to find out," said Zack.

Had the envelope not been sealed, I wouldn't have given a second thought to opening it. After all, Lupe had entrusted us with the contents of the suitcase. Still, I hesitated. Nothing else we'd come across so far had been sealed, let alone addressed to someone. And not only was the envelope sealed and addressed, it was hidden in the lid pocket, as if the person who had placed it there wasn't quite sure she wanted it discovered.

I placed the envelope on the table and closed the suitcase. "I think we should let Lupe open it. I'll call her tomorrow."

FOUR

I arrived at work the next morning to find enough baked goods in the break room to fill a small bakery. When Cloris can't sleep, she bakes. Looking around at the vast assortment of muffins, coffeecakes, turnovers, and pastries spread out across the counter and table, I knew she'd pulled an all-nighter. I piled an assortment of muffins onto a large plate and grabbed two cups of coffee. Juggling everything, along with my purse and tote, I hurried down the hallway in search of the insomniac baker.

I found her pacing her cubicle. "Did you get any sleep last night?" I asked, even though I already knew the answer to my question from the evidence in the break room.

"I didn't even try."

I handed her one of the cups and placed the plate on the edge of her desk, taking note of the empty coffee cup and plate of crumbs next to her keyboard. Cloris would need a steady diet of sugar and caffeine to get her through the day. I dropped my purse and tote on her spare chair and shrugged out of my coat. "What did Gregg say?"

She grabbed a chocolate chip muffin and shoved half of it into her mouth. Around the mouthful she asked, "You want the G-rated short version or the complete four-letter rant?"

"Your choice." If Cloris needed to blow off steam with some X-rated language, I didn't mind acting as her sounding board. After all, what were friends for?

She shrugged. "I'll spare you the details. I'm too exhausted. Bottom line, we need to hire a lawyer, a shark who's willing to take our case on contingency."

"Do defense attorneys take cases on contingency?"

Cloris washed down her muffin with a swig of coffee before answering. "Gregg wants to counter-sue for slander. Or is it libel? I can never remember the difference, even when I've had a decent night's sleep."

"Do you have a lawyer in mind?"

"Not really. We've never filed a lawsuit. We've only used attorneys for real estate transactions and to draw up our wills."

I nibbled at the edges of an apricot and pistachio muffin, savoring every sweet morsel. Even while totally depressed and worried sick, Cloris created culinary masterpieces. Me? I prefer to roll up the windows of my car and scream at the top of my lungs. We all deal with stress in different ways.

"Zack said he'd talk to Patricia for you. As an assistant prosecutor, I'm sure she's worked across the aisle from many sharks. Some of them probably also practice in New Jersey."

She placed her hand over her mouth to cover a yawn. "I'd appreciate it."

I'd never seen Cloris so exhausted. She fought to keep her eyelids open. Usually I'm the one burning the proverbial candle at both ends, kept awake at night by financial worries. Massive doses of sugar and caffeine weren't going to cut it for her this morning. "What do you have on your schedule today?"

"Everything I didn't get done yesterday, plus what's on today's schedule."

"None of which you'll accomplish if you can't keep your eyes open. Come with me." I grabbed her hand and led her down the hall to my craft closet. I unlocked the door, switched on the light, and pulled her inside.

The closet, more a small room, is where I store supplies, models, and props for photo shoots. I'm the only one who uses it. Steel shelves run the length of the walls to the left and right. I opened one of the large plastic tubs lining a row of shelves and began tossing foam pillow forms onto the floor.

"What are you doing?" asked Cloris.

"Making a bed for you."

"But—"

I grabbed a bolt of plush fabric and spread it out over the pillows. The makeshift accommodation certainly wasn't on par with the Waldorf-Astoria, but Cloris would have a comfortable bed for a few quiet, uninterrupted hours of snooze time. "Don't argue with me. Lie down."

Cloris opened her mouth to protest again but took one look at the comfy bed I'd created for her and obeyed. I found a crocheted afghan in another tub and draped it over her. "Now go to sleep. I'll cover for you." I turned off the light and stepped out of the closet. I think she was sound asleep before I closed the door.

I headed back to Cloris's cubicle to retrieve my coat, purse, tote, coffee, and the remainder of the muffins, then crossed the hall into my own cubicle and settled in for the day. My work to-do list for the day contained quite a few items, but before I addressed any of them, I needed to phone Lupe.

I downed the remainder of my coffee and placed a call to her. She answered on the first ring. Once we dispensed with the usual pleasantries, I asked her if she had any other relatives named Lupe.

"My grandmother had a sister named Lupe. I was named for her. So was a cousin who lives in Florida."

"Anyone who might still be living in Cuba?"

"As far as I know, all my relatives made it out shortly after Castro came to power. Why?"

I explained about finding the sealed envelope and my reluctance to open it. "So far we've come across nothing else that's sealed. If this is personal, you should be the one to open it."

"I suppose, but why would something addressed to me be hidden in a suitcase brought over from Cuba decades before I was born?" She thought for a moment. "Maybe my grandparents had a friend named Lupe, and they were asked to hold onto some papers for her."

"Given the political turmoil back then, that's certainly a possibility."

"Do you have the envelope with you?"

"No, it's back at Zack's apartment."

"Feel free to open it when you get home tonight. Call me if it's important, but after all these years I can't imagine it would be."

Over the next few hours I ticked off a number of items on my to-do list. At one point, Naomi Dreyfus, our editorial director, popped into my cubicle. Naomi always amazed me. Even in the worst of situations, like the time a crazed madwoman was on her way to kill us, she never lost her cool. At fifty-nine her flawless patrician features remained free of wrinkles and worry lines, and

I'd never noticed a single strand of her silver tresses escape her trademark chignon. She looked as perfect at the end of the day as she did the moment she arrived at the office. Whatever her secret, she should bottle it. Women across America would stand in line to buy a case.

"I can't seem to find Cloris," she said. "Did she come in today?"

I am the world's worst liar. My face always contorts into an uncontrollable smirk, giving me away every time. I passed along the defective Fib Gene to Alex. Nick, on the other hand, inherited Karl's Look-You-in-the-Eye-and-Lie-With-a-Straight-Face gene. Luckily, at the moment I was standing with my back facing the entrance to my cubicle. Without turning around, I crossed my fingers and said, "I believe she had a meeting with a cookbook author."

"When she comes back, tell her I need to see her."

"Will do."

"How are you coming with your presentation for Monday?"

I turned and smiled, the need to lie having passed. "Polishing it up now."

"Good. I'll look forward to seeing what you've come up with." She waved, pivoted on her heels, and strode down the hall. Crisis averted.

I glanced at the clock on my computer. Four and a half hours had passed since I settled Cloris into the cozy nest I'd created for her in my supply closet. Since she hadn't returned to her cubicle in that time, hopefully she'd fallen sleep. I hated the idea of waking her, but with Naomi looking for her, I had no choice. Naomi was a great boss, but even she had her limits when it came to allowing her staff a certain amount of leeway. Sleeping on the job would cross even Naomi's line.

After making certain the coast was clear, I headed off to wake Cloris for lunch.

~*~

The remainder of the workday passed uneventfully. Cloris had caught enough shuteye that with a constant supply of caffeine and sugar the remainder of the day, no one suspected anything out of the norm. Not even Naomi who scheduled an impromptu meeting with her once Cloris returned from her fictitious interview with the cookbook author.

If only I could deal with the chaos of my home life the way I seamlessly managed the occasional monkey wrench tossed into my work life. Then again, our only work diva is our fashion editor, and she's no match for the likes of Mama and Lucille, the Betty Davis and Joan Crawford of the Garden State.

My dinner reprieves from those two weren't nearly as frequent as I wished, given that even Mama wouldn't eat her own cooking. Before Lawrence's arrest, he and Mama showed up to mooch dinner most nights. Apparently even my leftover tuna noodle casserole beats her burnt mystery meat hands-down.

With Lawrence behind bars, Mama continues to show up for meals nearly every night. I have no idea why we were spared her company the last two evenings, but it probably involved a new man in her life. No doubt Flora Sudberry Periwinkle Ramirez Scoffield Goldberg O'Keefe Tuttnauer was already on the prowl for Husband Number Seven.

I heard the shrill verbal exchange between Mama and Lucille as I stepped across the threshold into the kitchen. I would have turned around and walked back outside except that Mama spied me from where she and Lucille were sparring in the dining room. She abruptly stopped shouting at Lucille and marched into the kitchen.

"Anastasia, what's this I hear about you canceling Thanksgiving dinner at Ira's home? And after all that man has done for us. Would it kill you to spend a few hours with him?"

As much as Mama likes Zack, I think she secretly hoped I'd fall for my extremely wealthy half-brother-in-law. Emphasis on *wealthy*. However, even if I'd never met Zack and putting aside the lack of chemistry between Ira and me, I'd rather wind up sharing a cardboard box with Lucille and Devil Dog than become stepmother to his three spoiled brats.

I dropped my purse and tote onto the kitchen table and shrugged out of my coat. "Mama, I've spent more than a few hours with Ira over the past four and a half months. I need a break from his family drama. I've got enough of my own."

"What's that supposed to mean?"

I nodded in the direction of the dining room. "Really? I need to spell it out for you?"

She glanced over her shoulder to find Lucille standing in the doorway. With one hand on her hip, my mother-in-law precariously balanced her full weight on her cane. "Well, it's hardly *my* fault you're stuck with the likes of her!" said Mama. "Besides, I don't see what that has to do with Thanksgiving dinner. Ira is family."

There's family, and then there's family. Our connection to Ira fell more in the realm of six degrees of separation. Well, maybe not as many as six, but the bonds that connected us contained recently forged, slightly weak links. If it weren't for the fact that Ira was the spitting image of Karl, albeit a younger, thinner version with more hair, I would have requested a DNA test when he showed up at my door last July.

Ira owns a string of car dealerships and has more money than the average hedge fund manager. He bought his way into our lives, claiming he owed us for the mess his half-brother created, not that he even knew of Karl's or our existence at the time.

First he offered me a "family discount" when my rust bucket Hyundai died, and I couldn't afford a reliable replacement. Next he gave Alex a relatively new Jeep for his birthday. I really wrestled with that one, but in the end, I gave in to my son's pleas to keep the car. As much as I didn't want to be beholden to Ira, Alex having his own set of wheels considerably simplified my life. Call it my deal with the devil.

Most recently, after playing matchmaker to Lawrence and Mama, Ira presented them with a condo in Scotch Plains as a wedding gift. Because he hadn't transferred the title prior to Lawrence's arrest, the property wasn't seized under New Jersey's forfeiture law. Mama now lived mortgage-free. I suspect Lawrence also foots the bills for her condo fees, taxes, and utilities, as well as the Uber account she uses to jaunt around when she can't bum a ride from Alex or me.

"Mama, you're welcome to spend Thanksgiving with Ira and his kids. The rest of us are having dinner at Chez Catherine."

Mama's perfectly plucked eyebrows shot up toward her hairline. "Chez Catherine? You didn't tell me you'd won the lottery, dear."

"I didn't." I stepped over to the kitchen counter and switched the heat level on the chicken and vegetables in the slow cooker to *warm*. "It's Zack's treat."

"Well...in that case..."

"Humph!" said Lucille. "How typical of your selfishness, Anastasia!"

Selfishness? Because I didn't want to subject myself and everyone else to a day none of us would enjoy? Least of all my mother-in-law? "In what way am I being selfish? Don't tell me you want to spend Thanksgiving with Ira and his kids."

After walking out on Lucille, Karl's father eventually married a woman who would give birth to Ira. However, to this day Lucille insists Isidore Pollack was abducted by J. Edgar Hoover.

She harrumphed a second time. "Don't be ridiculous. I'm talking about waste and civic responsibility. That meal will cost enough to feed the county homeless for a week."

Hardly. Maybe a day or two but I would not allow Lucille to make me feel guilty for enjoying an expensive dinner in an upscale restaurant, not when her son's irresponsible—not to mention criminal—behavior had nearly put my sons and me out on the street.

"You're welcome to stay home and make yourself a ham sandwich if you don't want to join us," I said, knowing darned well—unfortunately—that Lucille's communist sensibilities would never prevent her from feasting on a gourmet meal prepared by a Cordon Bleu chef. "I'm sure Zack will be happy to donate the cost of your dinner to the local food pantry."

My mother-in-law lasered an evil eye at me before hobbling off toward the living room. I grabbed my coat and wrapped it around my shoulders.

"Where are you going?" asked Mama.

"I have to check on something Zack and I are working on."

"Is that what they're calling it now? I can't keep up with the latest jargon for a quickie."

"Mama! I'm not—"

She waved her hand in dismissal. "Don't be such a stick in the mud, dear. I know what's going on between the two of you."

I opened the back door. "I'll be back in exactly one minute."

"How I miss my youth! It now takes me a good five minutes to reach a satisfying—"

"TMI, Mama!" I slammed the door before she could finish her sentence.

I entered the apartment above my garage to find Zack at his computer while Alex and Nick worked on homework at the breakfast bar. "Too noisy in the house?" I asked.

"I'll say," said Nick.

"Are they both still alive?" asked Alex, referring to his grandmothers.

"They were when I left." Although at some point Mama and Lucille's animosity toward each other might result in a duel to the death. As the former social secretary of the Daughters of the American Revolution and a woman who claimed to trace her ancestry back to Russian nobility, Mama represented everything Lucille had opposed for most of her life. At least with Mama now ensconced in her condo, they were no longer sharing a bedroom under my roof.

"Dinner is ready," I told my sons. "Go wash up and set the table. Zack and I will be along shortly."

The boys gathered up their books. Once they left the apartment, I told Zack about my conversation with Mama. "I don't know whether to laugh or cry. The woman is incorrigible."

"Laugh," he said. "Between Flora and Lucille, you need to release as many endorphins as possible."

I couldn't help but chuckle. "Isn't that the truth?"

"I spoke with Lupe today," I said as I walked over to the table where we'd left the sealed envelope. "She suggested her grandmother might have been holding the envelope for a friend, perhaps even hiding it for someone, given the political climate back then.

"Certainly a possibility," said Zack.

I picked up the envelope and tapped it against the palm of my hand. "She gave me permission to open it."

Zack reached into his desk drawer, withdrew an antique ivory letter opener, and handed it to me. A row of miniature elephants marched along the back of the four-inch blade from the tip to the handle, which featured an elephant standing on a pedestal. "This is amazing. Where did you get it?"

"It belonged to my great-great-grandfather. It's from a mid-nineteenth century Chinese portable writing desk."

I continued to stare mesmerized at the letter opener, caressing the intricate carving.

"Ironic, isn't it?" asked Zack.

"What?"

"A majestic beast is slaughtered so that someone can immortalize its image in part of its body."

As a photojournalist, Zack had seen firsthand how poachers were decimating the elephant population. "Do you feel conflicted?"

"Absolutely." He stared at the letter opener for a moment before finally clearing his throat and pointing to the envelope.

"Right." I slipped the tip of the ivory under the flap and carefully ripped open the envelope. After handing the letter opener back to Zack, I pulled a folded sheet of paper from the envelope. As I unfolded it, an old Polaroid snapshot fluttered to the floor.

Zack stooped to retrieve the photo. "A newborn?" he asked,

showing it to me.

"I would think so." The baby in the picture looked no more than a day or two old.

Zack flipped over the photo to reveal a date. "Nearly fifty years ago," he said.

As I began to read the letter, I quickly realized the contents were indeed meant for Lupe. "Oh, my!"

FIVE

The letter was written several years ago. As I began to read aloud, tears clouded my vision and clogged my throat:

My Darling Lupe,

If you're reading this, you've found the suitcase of photos and papers my parents brought with them from Cuba. My thought was that at some point you'd want to sort through the items and would come across this letter. What I'm about to tell you, even your father never knew. Now that he's gone, I can tell you what I've told no one in all these years. Attitudes may have changed over the decades, but my guilt over what happened will always hold the truth captive while I'm alive.

When I was fourteen, I made a terrible mistake, bringing shame upon my family. The infant in the photograph is the result of that mistake. When I realized I was pregnant, my parents sent me away to give birth, telling family and friends I had won a one-semester scholarship to a prestigious girls' academy in upstate New York. In reality the "academy" was a Catholic home for unwed mothers.

I was only allowed to hold your sister for a few minutes before she was whisked from my arms and given to the couple adopting her. I never knew their name.

I shouldn't even have this photo. A kindly nun slipped into the nursery with her camera, snapped the Polaroid, and handed it to me before I left the hospital. She said she felt sorry for me and the other girls forced to give up our babies, and that we at least deserved to have a photo to keep their memories alive. I'll forever be grateful for her understanding and her defiant act.

By this point tears streamed down my cheeks. Sadness so overwhelmed me that I couldn't continue reading. I handed the letter to Zack. He continued:

Why, you might wonder, am I divulging this to you now, after my death? It's because I don't want your sister's memory to die with me. Someone needs to know that even with what happened to me, I loved that little baby girl the moment I set eyes on her, and not a day has gone by that I haven't thought about her.

Also, at some point in the future she might track you down. I've lived for years—part hoping and part fearing—she might find me. If she does, please tell her that giving her up was the hardest thing I ever had to do and that I hope she's had a wonderful life with her adoptive parents.

And always know how much I have loved you.
Your Mami

Zack folded the letter and placed it and the photo of the baby back into the envelope. "Are you up to calling Lupe?"

I swiped my tear-stained cheeks and blew my nose before

taking a deep breath and nodding. "This can't wait."

"Agreed."

I'd left my phone in my purse in the kitchen. Zack whipped his out of his pocket and handed it to me. When Lupe answered, I said, "Can you come over this evening?"

"Is it important?"

"It is."

I ended the call. Too overwhelmed with emotion, I walked silently hand-in-hand with Zack into the house.

~*~

I never expected Lupe to arrive so quickly. The doorbell rang before my first forkful of stew had made it halfway from my plate to my mouth.

"I'll get it," said Alex around a mouthful of food. He bolted from the table and raced to the front door.

"He's got a new girlfriend," Nick stage whispered.

"A *new* girlfriend?"

"He and Kayla broke up."

Kayla? Talk about being out of the loop! I wasn't aware my seventeen-year-old son ever had *any* girlfriend, let alone a new one. When did he squeeze a relationship into his over-scheduled life of sports, assorted extra-curricular activities, and part-time job? Not to mention homework, which I knew for a fact he completed each night, given his 4.0 GPA. Alex had planned to attend Harvard. Unfortunately, life, by way of his duplicitous father's death and its aftermath, had pulverized that dream. Given current finances, even community college would be a financial stretch.

"She works at Starbucks with him," continued Nick.

I hoped she wasn't the barista with chartreuse hair, pierced tongue, and hedgehog tattoos that covered her entire left arm. I also hoped that if the relationship had already progressed to a certain level, the two of them were not allowing their hormones to overrule their common sense. Alex had enough of an uphill battle ahead of him, and after reading Carmen's letter, the last thing I wanted to think about was the possibility of an unwanted pregnancy foisted upon two teenagers. Especially if one of those teenagers was my son.

Thankfully, Alex didn't return to the dining room with a chartreuse-haired, hedgehog-tattooed, tongue-pierced girlfriend in tow; he arrived with Lupe. She took one look at the dinner table and began to stammer. "I...Anastasia, I'm sorry. I thought you'd be finished with dinner by now. Should I come back later?"

"Don't be silly, Lupe."

Zack rose and offered Lupe his seat before dragging one of the kitchen chairs into the dining room.

"Would you like some stew?" I asked.

She shook her head as she shrugged out of her coat and draped it across the back of the chair. "Thanks, I've already eaten. Your call sounded so urgent. Does this have anything to do with the envelope you found?"

"What envelope, dear?" asked Mama. I swear the woman could smell a juicy story a mile away.

Zack and I exchanged a quick glance. "Nothing, Mama."

Mama smacked her fork onto the side of her plate. "Anastasia, when will you learn that I can always tell when you're lying to me?"

Busted! I sighed. "This doesn't concern you, Mama." Not that she cared. Mama thrived on gossip. We had a saying in our family: Tell Flora; tell the world. More than once I'd had to threaten her with banishment from my home to keep her tongue from wagging. No way was I telling her anything about Carmen's letter to Lupe.

"That's never stopped her before," said Lucille around a mouthful of food. "That one sticks her nose into everyone's business." She stabbed a piece of carrot and glared at Mama as she shoved the vegetable into her already packed mouth.

Mama slammed her fists on either side of her plate, rattling the silverware and causing the water to slosh around precariously close to the rims of our glasses. "You keep out of this, you...you...you freeloading communist! No one asked for your opinion."

Behind me Ralph emitted a loud squawk. I turned to find him perched atop the breakfront. "*You are now sailed into the north of my lady's opinion; where you will hang like an icicle on a Dutchman's beard. Twelfth Night.* Act Three, Scene Two."

"Or yours," said Lucille.

I didn't know if she meant Ralph or Mama, but it hardly mattered. I'd had enough. "Lupe, let's talk in Zack's apartment." I rose, grabbed my plate, and silently indicated to Zack to do the same as Lupe slipped back into her coat.

"Well, this is all rather cloak and dagger," said Mama.

"No, just none of your business," I muttered.

"What did you say, dear? I didn't quite catch that."

Quite being the operative word. Mama's eyes told me she'd heard every word loud and clear. She was either deliberately acting clueless or had decided to resort to sarcasm. Either way, I refused to bite. Ignoring her, I strode from the dining room and headed toward the back door. Lupe and Zack followed.

The bone-chilling wind that had descended over the area since I'd arrived home had now reached near-sub-zero levels. Winter didn't seem to want to wait until its official arrival date this year. Neither Zack nor I had grabbed our coats before leaving the house. In the time it took us to cover the short distance between the back door and the entrance to the apartment, our dinners had gone from steamy to ice cold. My limbs hovered mere degrees above frostbite.

Note to self: no matter how angry you get, always check the weather before storming out of the house.

Once inside the apartment, I glanced at Zack as I rubbed feeling back into my arms. Unlike me, he didn't appear fazed by the freezing temperatures. He took my plate and placed both of our dinners into the microwave to zap some warmth back into the food. While the stew reheated, he poured three glasses of wine and placed them on the coffee table.

I walked across the room to retrieve Carmen's letter. "You should sit down to read this," I told Lupe as I handed the envelope to her.

She emitted a nervous laugh. "Your mother is right. This seems very cloak and dagger."

"It is a bit of a mystery," I said.

Ignoring my advice, Lupe remained standing as she removed the contents of the envelope. "Who is this?" she asked, staring at the photo of the infant.

"The letter will explain," I said.

Lupe unfolded the single sheet of stationery and began to read. Only the beeping of the microwave broke the silence in the room. Zack and I ignored it as we focused on Lupe. Her hand soon began to shake and her knees buckled. She reached for the arm of the nearest chair and collapsed into the seat. "I have a sister?"

I nodded. "Apparently so."

"This doesn't make sense. I never remember any talk of a baby, no whispered conversations behind closed doors, nothing that would have piqued my curiosity. Surely, I would have heard some rumor over the years."

"It sounds like your mother only told your grandparents, and they went to great lengths to keep the rest of the family from learning about the pregnancy," I said.

"But what about the baby's father?" asked Lupe. "I can't believe my grandparents wouldn't have confronted him and his parents."

"Not if they wanted to contain the fallout and protect your mother from scandal," said Zack. "Times were different back then. It's possible the father never knew about the pregnancy."

Lupe's initial shock gave way to anger. "I can't believe Mami kept this from me. I grew up wanting a sister. When she'd ask me what I wanted for Christmas or my birthday, I'd always say a baby sister. She told me that was in God's hands, not hers. Yet all along she knew I had a sister somewhere?"

"How could she have told you?" I asked. "You were a child."

"Besides," said Zack, "according to her letter, your father didn't even know."

Lupe's anger segued into a steely determination. "As close as Mami was with her aunts and cousins, I find it hard to believe she didn't confide in at least one of them. I need to know what happened."

"What will you do?" I asked.

She rose from the chair and shoved the letter and photo into her purse. "Thursday is Thanksgiving. All my relatives will be gathered together. What better time to shake a few of the branches on our family tree and see what secrets fall loose?"

Horrified, I pictured the scenario: Lupe's nuclear family suffering a nuclear meltdown over turkey and stuffing. "Surely you're not going to confront everyone over Thanksgiving dinner?"

"Why not? Everyone will be there."

"Do you think that's the best approach?"

Lupe grew defensive. "Absolutely. That way even if no one comes forward with information, I'll be able to gauge everyone's reactions to see who's hiding something."

And I thought dinners at Casa Pollack often grew explosive! I couldn't see how such a confrontation would end well, let alone give her the answers she sought. Someone had to talk some sense into her, but I couldn't find the words to dissuade her.

I looked to Zack for help. He came to my rescue. "If some of your relatives do know the truth," he said, "they may feel honor bound to keep your mother's secret from you."

"I don't care," said Lupe. An angry red color suffused her neck and face. Her voice trembled. "I have a right to know."

I rose from the sofa, walked over to where she sat, and perched on the edge of the coffee table. Tears had begun to cascade down Lupe's cheeks. Leaning forward, I pried her hands from the chair and held them in both of mine. "Agreed. But think this through for a moment. Maybe confronting everyone over Thanksgiving dinner isn't the best way to get someone to open up about the past."

"And what about your children?" added Zack. "And the other children who will be at the dinner? For now this is a conversation for adult ears only."

Lupe frowned as our words sunk in, and she began to realize the chaos her plan would unleash. She swiped at her face with her sleeve and sniffed back a fresh batch of tears threatening to spill from her eyes. "I suppose I am being rash." Then she laughed nervously. "Maybe confronting everyone over cranberry sauce and sweet potato casserole isn't the best approach."

I exhaled a deep breath. "Under the circumstances, I think you should start with some private, one-on-one conversations."

Lupe nodded. "With Mami now gone, I should be able to wheedle the truth out of at least one of my relatives." She grew silent for a moment, appearing to weigh her options. Finally, she continued, "And I think I know just the person to target."

"Who?" I asked.

"My great-aunt Renata. She was my grandmother's older sister."

I remembered Renata, the frail but feisty ninety-something matriarch of the family, from Carmen's funeral. Her relatives had withheld from her the circumstances surrounding Carmen's death, telling her only that Carmen had died from heart failure. They deliberately left out the part about the heart failure being the result of an assassin's knife.

Although, given the state of Renata's health, maybe she wasn't the best person for Lupe to confront about Carmen's secret pregnancy. Whether Renata knew anything or not, the shock of Lupe confronting her about it might not go well. But a private conversation with an elderly great-aunt was far less volatile than Lupe's initial plan of attack.

"When will you speak with her?" I asked, hoping she wasn't considering pulling Renata aside to confront her on Thursday. The consequences of that might be as bad as blurting something out at the dinner table.

Lupe took a shaky breath before standing. "Friday. I'm off from work. I'll pay her a visit in the morning."

As she stepped out of the apartment onto the landing, she hesitated, then turned, and asked, "Anastasia, are you working on Friday?"

I shook my head.

"Would you come with me to visit Aunt Renata? I could use the support."

Under the circumstances, how could I refuse?

SIX

I closed the door behind Lupe, then collapsed onto the sofa while Zack set the microwave to heat up our dinners for a second time. Neither of us spoke as the timer counted down the seconds. When the microwave beeped, he removed the plates and brought them over to the coffee table.

I took one look at what had once passed as meat, potatoes, carrots, and onions and pushed the dish aside. After spending all day in the slow cooker and twice zapped in the microwave, the stew now looked as appetizing as a week-old airline meal—the kind served in coach. On a cut-rate carrier.

Zack removed both plates to the kitchen and rummaged in the refrigerator and pantry. He returned with an assortment of cheeses, a box of crackers, and a bowl of grapes. After settling beside me, he asked, "Better?"

"The food or me?"

"Both."

I separated a grape from the bunch and popped it into my

mouth. "At least this looks and tastes like food."

"Always a plus. And you?"

I drained my wine glass and held it out for a refill. "Feeling guilty."

"Haven't we already had this discussion?"

I nodded. "This is different. I'm feeling guilty over feeling selfish. I have enough drama in my life. I really don't want to be part of Lupe's family drama."

"Then why did you agree to go with her Friday?"

"That goes back to the other guilt."

Zack frowned at me.

I knew my feelings were justified, though. "No matter what you say, if I hadn't set in motion the circumstances surrounding Carmen's murder, Lupe wouldn't have discovered the suitcase, I wouldn't have found the letter, and I wouldn't have agreed to go with her to speak with her great-aunt."

"Not necessarily," he said.

"You're wrong. Each event led directly to the next one in a chain that began with my suspicions over Cynthia's death."

"By that reasoning you might as well blame Ira for her death."

"Ira? How?"

"He introduced Flora to Lawrence. Hell, why not blame Lucille? Ira wouldn't even exist if she hadn't ended her relationship with his father."

"Now you're really being ridiculous."

"Am I? The point is, we have no way of knowing that Carmen wouldn't have died anyway."

"That makes no sense, Zack. She wouldn't have been murdered if I—"

"I didn't say murdered. We all die at some point. If Carmen

died of a heart attack that day—"

"But she didn't!"

"You don't know that she wouldn't have. Or suffered a stroke. Or been attacked by a rabid raccoon."

"A rabid raccoon? Really, Zack? How likely is that?"

"The point is that no matter when Carmen died or how, Lupe still would have eventually found the suitcase and asked you to create albums for her kids. Maybe not this week or the next or next month or next year, but at some point in the future someone— you or me or Lupe—would have found that letter."

His reasoning smacked of grasping at straws, but I conceded his point. "Even so, I would have much preferred to deal with this in the distant future. Preferably without a murder and when my life contained far less chaos."

"Agreed. But at least we talked Lupe out of confronting her entire family over Thanksgiving."

"A small victory." I laughed in spite of myself. "Can you imagine the can of worms she would have let loose?"

"Forget the worms," said Zack. "Think more along the lines of an exploding twenty-gallon drum of vipers."

Which was why I wanted nothing to do with unearthing the truth behind the long-buried Cordova family secret. Yet here I was, now firmly entrenched in the muck, thanks to my inability to say no to Lupe Cordova Betancourt.

~*~

I'd completely forgotten Wednesday was the day before Thanksgiving. Typical New Jersey drive-time gridlock is bad enough but the day before a major holiday? *Fuhgeddaboudit!* After sitting bumper-to-bumper with travelers getting an early morning jump on holiday traffic (ha!), shoppers rushing to pick up their turkeys, and those of us just trying to get to work, I finally arrived at the office forty minutes late.

Luckily, no one noticed because no one was around. Most of my coworkers had taken a vacation day to spend cooking, baking, or traveling. I used to enjoy days like this, when I was one of only a handful of people not off on assignment, vacation, or taking a sick day. It's amazing how much you can accomplish when your day is free of distractions and interruptions. But that all changed one evening last year when after returning to the office to catch up on some work, I discovered a dead body glued to my desk chair. Now the sound of only my heels clicking along the empty halls sets off a massive case of the heebie-jeebies in me.

I regretted not taking the day off. I was all caught up on my work. I didn't have to cook for Thanksgiving. Anyone else would have jumped at the chance for a mental health day, but in truth, my mental health fared far better alone at work than stuck at home with Lucille and the Daughters of the October Revolution, heebie-jeebies notwithstanding.

I dumped my purse and coat in my cubicle and headed for the break room to start a pot of coffee, only to find I wasn't quite alone. Cloris stood at the counter, measuring coffee grounds into the pot.

"I thought I was the only one who showed up today," I said, zeroing in on the plastic container next to the coffee pot. I lifted the lid to find ten pumpkin muffins.

"I've been here since six this morning," she said.

I suppose that accounted for the muffins being two shy of a dozen. I grabbed one as I settled into a chair. "Why?"

Cloris poured a carafe of cold water into the coffee maker and flipped the switch before joining me at the table. "I couldn't sleep, and since I've gotten next to no work done all week, thanks to that lawsuit, I still have to proof copy for the issue in production and finish up my presentation for Monday's editorial meeting."

Given the muffins, I suspected Cloris had again spent at least part of the night stress baking. I took a bite of muffin and along with pumpkin, tasted chunks of apple. If only I could harness my own stress in such a productive manner. Then again, the added pounds I'd pack on from stress eating after stress baking would only increase my stress levels, not alleviate them.

"Any news?" I asked.

"We hired a lawyer last night. He agreed with Gregg about filing a countersuit."

"For what?"

"Basically the kitchen sink. Defamation of character. Slander. Libel. Fraud. You name it. We'd better win. You have any idea what lawyers charge by the hour?"

"A bundle."

"I'll see your bundle and raise you tenfold. And we'll have to pay it if we don't win the counter-suit."

"Ouch."

"Yeah." She reached for a muffin. "We also spoke with the police. They're initiating an investigation."

"Didn't the new owners call the police when they first received the letters?"

Cloris bit into the muffin and shook her head. "The police said they have no record of a report."

"That in itself sounds suspicious."

"Probably because the letters don't exist. They didn't include copies in the lawsuit, just summaries and some quoted text. The lawyer is demanding to see the actual letters."

I knew this from the Internet search Zack and I had done. What I didn't know, since I'd never found myself on the receiving end of a lawsuit—thank goodness— was whether including copies of the evidence was standard procedure or not. I scanned my memory for episodes of all the legal TV shows I'd watched over the years that included scenes where one character slapped an envelope into the hand of another character and said, "You've been served." I came up empty. Not that it would have helped since I knew Hollywood took massive liberties for dramatic effect.

Still, had someone sent me threatening letters, my first instinct would be to call the police, not a litigator. Couple that with the new owners waiting until they'd spent tens of thousands of dollars on renovations before deciding the letters prevented them from moving into the house, and it all smacked of a scam. "What do you know about the new owners?" I asked.

Cloris got up to pour us both cups of coffee. "Not much other than they came from somewhere in the Midwest." She thought for a moment as she carried the cups back to the table. "Wisconsin, maybe? Or Minnesota?" She shrugged. "They qualified for a mortgage. That was all we cared about at the time. We didn't meet them until settlement."

"Did you have any conversation with them?"

"Not much. They weren't chatty. We said we hoped they loved the house as much as we had. They said it was perfect, exactly what they wanted, which is kind of odd, given that they proceeded to do a massive renovation. Anyway, once we finished up the paperwork, they handed over a check, we handed over the keys, and that was that. We went our separate ways."

Although the law firm would certainly look into the buyers' background during the course of preparing the counter-lawsuit, perhaps I could save Cloris and Gregg some of those "bundle times ten" billable hours with a bit of Googling. I suspected the police would also investigate the buyers, given that one plus one definitely wasn't adding up to two, but it couldn't hurt to have ten additional digits tripping across the keyboard and clicking on whatever links turned up in a search.

Between that and working on Lupe's scrapbook, I'd filled my to-do list for the day. But not wanting to raise Cloris's hopes, only to dash them should my cyber-detecting fail, I kept my plan to myself. I'd present my search results only if I uncovered something useful.

I decided to tackle Cloris's problem first. In all the online articles Zack and I had discovered about The Sentinel and the lawsuit, none had gone into any depth about the new owners. Most seemed more interested in the sensationalism of what had been dubbed The Sentinel House than the people involved in the lawsuit. Several articles mentioned both the new owners and the former owners had declined requests for interviews, referring reporters to their respective attorneys.

Cloris hadn't mentioned hearing from any reporters, but maybe she and Gregg weren't answering their phone. If I were in her shoes, I'd certainly let all calls go to voicemail the way I did any unfamiliar number. As far as I was concerned, the person who had invented Caller ID deserved a Nobel Prize.

However, after two hours of online searching, my knowledge of the new owners hadn't increased one iota, but my frustration level had grown considerably.

I suppose I should have expected not to find anything definitive, given their extremely common names. I first scoured social media, but if the John and Susan Jones I searched for had

Facebook, Twitter, or Instagram accounts, they had enabled ultra-strict privacy settings, or shut down their accounts when they filed the lawsuit. None of the accounts that popped up pointed to the people who bought Cloris's house, only a myriad of other people by the same name.

When I ran a Google search, tens of thousands of hits appeared. With no other information about the couple besides their names and the contents of the lawsuit, narrowing down the search parameters proved futile. Plodding through the massive number of links from my initial search would take days, if not weeks. As much as I wanted to help Cloris, I didn't have that kind of time.

Although, as I stared at the computer screen, my mind raced with other possibilities. What if John and Susan Jones were aliases? But why? Several possibilities sprang to mind—celebrities who wanted to maintain a certain level of privacy, people in Witness Protection, or grifters running a scam.

I immediately discounted the celebrity theory. If either John or Susan Jones were a celebrity, Cloris would have recognized them. And if not Cloris, certainly someone at the attorney's office during closing, or one of the news services that had run with the story would have ferreted out such explosive information.

As for Witness Protection, I knew something about the program. Our former fashion editor had been placed in WitSec when she agreed to testify against her mobster father and boyfriend. Not only did people in WitSec have to keep a low profile, they had to remain squeaky clean to stay in the program. If the new owners were in Witness Protection, wouldn't the U.S. Marshals prevent them from filing a lawsuit that would open them up to all sorts of scrutiny?

I also knew a bit about grifters. An elderly neighbor had fallen victim to one not too long ago. Of the three choices, in my non-professional opinion, the grifter option appeared the most likely.

I wondered if their lawyer was in on it.

Then again, from what I'd learned about grifters, they usually had a take-the-money-and-run M.O. Lawsuits take years to wind their way through the courts. The longer the con lasts, the more likely the risk of exposure. These people hadn't approached Cloris and Gregg to demand any sort of restitution. There was no attempt at a shakedown. They'd skipped Go and gone directly to Lawsuit. I reluctantly came to the conclusion that pegging the new buyers as grifters also made no sense.

So who were these people, and what was their motive? Could there really be a Sentinel?

SEVEN

Lupe picked me up at ten o'clock Friday morning. "How was your Thanksgiving?" she asked after I settled myself in her car.

"Relaxing."

She raised both eyebrows. "Is that sarcasm?"

"No. Zack took us out to dinner. No shopping, no cooking, no cleanup. And no Lucille." I never expected my mother-in-law to pass up a free dinner at a fancy French restaurant, but that's exactly what she did, going off on a rant about bourgeoisie excess and children starving in Africa. Zack told her he'd make a contribution to the Red Cross to help with the famine epidemic, but she still refused to join us, opting instead to dine alone on leftover meatloaf. "Best Thanksgiving ever."

"Lucky you. With Mami gone, hosting fell to me. We had over two-dozen relatives descend on us. We split up the cooking, and I had lots of help with the dishes, but as you can imagine, I wasn't in the best of moods. I kept staring at various relatives, wondering which ones knew about my sister."

I patted her hand. "Maybe we'll get some answers from your aunt."

Lupe's great-aunt lived with her widowed daughter Elena in a two-bedroom apartment complex for active seniors in Cranford, one town over from Westfield. Renata hardly qualified as active at this point in her life, spending much of her day confined to a wheelchair, but according to Lupe, she was too stubborn to move into an assisted living facility.

"Elena cares for her mother by herself?" I asked, dreading the day when Mama would no longer be self-sufficient. What would I do? I couldn't give up my job to care for her, but neither one of us had the financial resources to move her into a quality assisted living facility. So I continually implored the Goddess of Older Parents to keep Mama healthy in both body and mind.

I also pleaded on behalf of Lucille. As much as I hated having her under my roof, I wasn't nasty enough to wish her into a Medicaid nursing home.

Not that she appreciated the sacrifices I've made for her. The communist pain in my patootie continues to insist I'm responsible for her son's death and its financially disastrous aftermath. If she only knew the truth...But knowing she'd never believe me, I've remained mum to spare myself the aggravation.

"At some point Elena will have to make some hard decisions about her mother," said Lupe. "After all, she's not exactly young, either."

"How old is she?"

"The same age as Mami."

"Were they close?"

Lupe slowed for a red light, turning toward me once the car came to a stop. "They're...were...first cousins. Renata was my grandmother's older sister. Mami and Elena were always on good terms, but as for hanging out together as teens?" She shrugged. "No one ever mentioned anything."

A few minutes later Lupe pulled into a parking space in front of a modern brick apartment complex. The building, landscaped with hibernating azaleas and rhododendrons, formed a horseshoe around a grassy expanse dotted with skeletal oaks and maples and a few pine trees. Wrought iron and wood benches sat randomly grouped under many of the trees.

A shopping complex that housed a supermarket, bank, pharmacy, and coffee shop was situated directly across the street, next to a two-story office building that contained an urgent care center on the ground floor and doctors' offices on the second floor. The gothic spire of the local Catholic Church rose up from a block behind the shops. A street sign at the corner indicated the location of the public library around the block. With so many of life's necessities within a short walk, the neighborhood was ideal for seniors—or anyone else who hated driving everywhere.

Lupe led me along a path that cut through the center of the horseshoe. A stinging wind sent the occasional burst of snowflakes from steel gray clouds dancing around us as we scurried to the main entrance of the complex.

Once inside the lobby, Lupe approached a security guard seated behind a wood and granite counter positioned halfway between the entrance and a bank of three elevators. A name plaque on the counter identified him as Officer Brummer. The badge pinned to his blue shirt read Garden State Security. "Lupe Betancourt to see Elena Telasco. She's expecting me."

He extended a pudgy hand. "I'll need to see ID." Lupe pulled out her license and placed it in his palm. "You, too," he said, indicating me with a sideways thrust of his salt and pepper stubbly chin.

I removed my license from my wallet and placed it on top of Lupe's in his still outstretched hand. He consulted his computer screen, then scanned our IDs. After returning the licenses, he called to alert Elena of our arrival. As he hung up the phone, he nodded toward the elevators behind him. "Second floor. Make a left out of the elevator. It's the third apartment on your right. Two-twenty-four."

Elena greeted us at her door. As soon as I saw her, I remembered her from Carmen's funeral. She had sung a moving tribute to her cousin. Given the circumstances, the coward in me had voted for skipping the service, but my conscience, spurred on by Zack's urging, had won out. However, the moment Elena's soaring soprano filled the church, I lost the battle to ward off my tears. I wasn't alone. By the time Elena finished singing "You'll Never Walk Alone," the entire congregation was dabbing at their eyes and blowing their noses.

After ushering us into the apartment, Elena took our coats and hung them in a closet near the front door. "I didn't realize you were bringing anyone with you, Lupe. I thought you wanted to speak with my mother."

"I do. This is Mami's neighbor Anastasia Pollack. She's helping me solve a mystery we've uncovered." Lupe then addressed me. "Anastasia, meet Mami's cousin Elena Telasco."

I held out my hand. "Pleased to meet you."

"And you," said Elena as she shook my hand, then turned back to Lupe. "What sort of mystery?"

"One that your mother might have answers to."

"Or at least be able to fill in some blanks," I added.

Elena shrugged. "I can't imagine how Mami could assist you in anything, but she's in the kitchen. I've made a fresh pot of coffee."

We followed Elena down the hall into a bright white and stainless steel kitchen so immaculate only the tantalizing scent of freshly baked tres leches cake filling the apartment proved someone made use of more than the microwave. The entire kitchen sparkled like a showroom display with not a stray crumb in sight or a single dirty dish left in the sink. If I'd just baked a cake, my kitchen would look like the aftermath of a food fight. Come to think of it, thanks to Mama, Lucille, and two teenage boys, my kitchen usually looked like the aftermath of a food fight, whether or not any baking had occurred.

The cake, along with plates, forks, and napkins, filled the middle of a polished oak table in the breakfast nook. Renata sat at the table, nearly swallowed up by her wheelchair. Although the temperature in the room hovered only a degree or two below sweltering, she wore a heavy black crocheted shawl draped around her shoulders. The severe white bun secured tightly at the nape of her neck did little to reduce the deep roadmap of wrinkles crisscrossing her face, but behind those ravages of age I discerned hints of a once elegant woman, an older version of the daughter who now cared for her.

According to Lupe, Renata suffered from both severe arthritis and diabetes and could barely walk, but her frail body did little to mask the clarity and intelligence emanating from two hawk-like, crystal blue eyes that spoke of a northern Spanish ancestry. I sincerely doubted even the most insignificant detail ever escaped the woman.

She raised both eyebrows over the rim of the coffee cup she held with both gnarled hands. Blue veins bulged beneath her paper-thin skin. When Elena introduced me and explained the reason for our visit, Renata gestured to the two chairs across from the table and said, "Sit."

Lupe and I settled in at the table. Elena poured coffee for us and took the seat next to her mother. Without asking if we'd like any, she began slicing the cake and passing it around.

No one had to twist my arm. My taste buds had kicked into overdrive the moment I'd entered the apartment. When it came to sweets, my willpower took off for parts unknown. I grabbed my fork and savored a mouthful of shear bliss. Elena's cake rivaled any Cloris had ever baked, but in a head-to-head competition that included ending with a spotless kitchen, Elena would win hands-down.

"We spent all day together yesterday, Lupe," said Renata. "What could possibly have happened since then that you need to talk about?"

Lupe took her time stirring milk and sugar into her cup, then took a sip before placing the cup back on its saucer before answering. "I wanted to speak with you in private, not in front of other family members."

"So you brought your friend? What could you possibly say in front of her that you couldn't say in front of the family?"

"While cleaning out Mami's house, I discovered a suitcase of old family photos in the attic."

Renata glanced at me. "What's that got to do with your friend?"

"Anastasia was Mami's neighbor. You met her at the funeral."

Renata studied me, as if searching her memory, then nodded in my direction. "Yes, I remember you now."

"Anastasia is a craft editor at a magazine," said Lupe. "I asked her to make albums from the photos for my children."

"And you want to know who the people in the photographs are?" asked Elena.

Lupe shook her head. "No, most of the photos are labeled."

"Then what?"

Lupe opened her purse and withdrew the envelope. "This was hidden in the suitcase. It's a letter from Mami addressed to me. She wrote it several years ago." Lupe passed the envelope across the table.

A pair of black frame glasses hung from a chain around Renata's neck. With shaking hands, she settled them onto her nose before picking up the envelope with Lupe's name written on it. As she fumbled to remove the single sheet of paper inside, the snapshot of the newborn fell out, face up, onto the table.

Elena lifted the photo and stared at it while her mother silently read the letter. I thought I noticed Elena's lower lip tremble for a split second, but she quickly scooped up a forkful of cake, shoved it in her mouth, and began chewing. Maybe I was mistaken. Or maybe not, given the faraway expression that had settled across her features as she continued to stare at the baby in the photograph. Perhaps she was the relative we should question about Carmen's baby, not her mother.

"Did you know?" Lupe asked her great-aunt.

Renata grabbed the photo from her daughter's hand. Without glancing at it, she shoved it, the letter, and the envelope back at Lupe. Indignation suffused her face and colored her words as she spoke. "Of course not."

"There's nothing you can tell me?" asked Lupe.

Behind her glasses Renata's eyes narrowed into slits. "I told you I don't know anything." She then turned to Elena and said, "I'm tired. Please show our guests out."

Lupe and I looked at each other. Renata definitely knew something, but she'd probably take whatever information she had with her to her grave. We rose, leaving our half-eaten cake and half-drunk coffee, and followed Elena back to the apartment's entrance. As we put on our coats, Elena whispered something in Lupe's ear.

"What did she say to you," I asked after the door shut behind us.

"She wants us to meet her at the coffee shop across the street. She'll come as soon as she settles Renata down for a morning nap."

I was now more convinced than ever that I hadn't imagined Elena's lip quiver when she looked at the photo of Carmen's baby.

Lupe and I walked across the street to the coffee shop. With so many people off from work today and schools closed for the Thanksgiving holiday, the place was jam-packed. A long line of customers, mostly teenagers, snaked from the counter nearly to the door. I spied an empty table toward the back of the café and made a beeline toward it to claim it for us while Lupe queued up to place our order.

Elena arrived just as Lupe had inched her way to the front of the line. She waited with her while the barista made our drinks. Then the two of them joined me at the table. They both took off their coats and draped them across the backs of their chairs before taking their seats.

No one spoke while Elena fidgeted with a packet of sugar and spent an inordinate amount of time stirring the sweetener into her coffee. All the while she kept her head down, avoiding eye contact with her niece. Lupe sat on the edge of her seat, her eyes shifting from me to her aunt, impatiently waiting for Elena to speak.

Elena continued to avoid the subject. She finally raised her head and opened her mouth but instead of speaking, she raised her cup to her mouth and sipped at her coffee.

I'd had enough. I cleared my throat. When she turned to look at me, I said, "Out with it."

She placed her cup back on the table, took a deep breath, and forced out a huge sigh as she nodded. "What I'm about to tell you is a secret I've kept for half a century."

EIGHT

"Carmen and I were not only cousins," Elena began. "We were the best of friends. Even though we lived in different towns, we went to the same Catholic school and often spent overnights at each other's home from the time we were five or six years old. One night when we were fourteen, we made a mistake that changed our lives forever." She paused for a moment, looking unsure about continuing. Finally, she sighed heavily before adding, "Carmen's life far worse than mine."

I didn't need a crystal ball to see into the future—or in this case, the past—to know Elena's tale would end with Carmen getting pregnant that night.

Lupe and I leaned forward, straining to hear Elena's soft voice, little more than a whisper, over the din of the crowded coffee shop. "What happened that night?" prodded Lupe.

Elena took a few sips of coffee, stalling another few seconds before continuing. "We had only recently entered our freshman year of high school. One of my classmates invited me to a party her brother was throwing that Saturday night. He was a senior and on the football team. Their parents were going out of town for the weekend and leaving their kids home alone. I asked if I could bring Carmen, and she agreed."

"Your parents didn't know about the party, did they?" I asked.

Elena shook her head. "They never would have let us go. They were very strict. We weren't even allowed to date yet." She lowered her head and stared into her coffee. "Carmen and I both chafed at our parents' old-world ways. They kept us from having fun. Nothing was going to stop us from attending that party. We were very naïve."

Or stupid.

"Carmen spent Saturday night at my house," she continued. "My family lived in Clark back then, Carmen in Union. We told my parents we wanted to go to a movie. My father dropped us off at the theater, but as soon as he drove away, we walked the few blocks to the address of the party. When we arrived, we discovered the party wasn't what we'd expected."

"What do you mean?" asked Lupe.

"There were five boys, all seniors, and the sister of one of them. She was the classmate who'd invited us. We knew we should leave, but she begged us to stay to help even out the boy/girl ratio until some other girls arrived. Because she looked so nervous, we agreed."

Elena scowled and shook her head before continuing. "She led us into the living room and introduced us to the boys. Someone handed us drinks. That was the last thing either Carmen or I remembered before we woke up half-naked on the floor in a darkened basement rec room. Our blouses were open, our bras undone, our skirts hiked up, our underpants missing."

Lupe's jaw dropped. "My mother was raped? That's how she got pregnant?"

Elena nodded. Tears spilled down her cheeks. She grabbed a napkin, swiped the tears from her face, then blew her nose.

"What did you do?" I asked.

"The only thing we could do. We straightened out our clothes, sneaked out of the house, and walked back to the theater."

"You didn't tell anyone?" asked Lupe.

Elena shook her head. "We felt too ashamed, not to mention guilty as hell. Things like that didn't happen to good girls."

I reached across the table and placed my hand over Elena's. "What happened wasn't your fault."

"In a way it was," she said. "We never should have gone to that party. We were asking for trouble."

"So you just went home and pretended nothing happened?" asked Lupe.

"I did call the police," said Elena, "before calling my father to pick us up."

I was confused. "So, you did report the rape?"

"No, I pretended to be a neighbor and complained about loud music and underage drinking going on at the house."

"Were the party-goers arrested?" I asked.

She snorted. "Of course not. Rumor had it they were hauled off to the station, and their parents had to come get them, but no charges were filed."

"Why not?" asked Lupe.

Elena shrugged. "Times were different back then. People didn't take underage drinking as seriously as they do today. I knew nothing would happen when I placed the call, but doing so made me feel better, at least for a few minutes. And I'll bet the girl who invited us and her brother wound up in a heap of trouble with their parents."

"But why didn't you report the rapes?" asked Lupe.

Elena sighed. "Like I said, times were different back then. These were boys from good families in a wealthy suburb. We were Cuban immigrants. No one would believe us. We'd be accused of making up a story. The scandal would destroy our families. We couldn't do that to our parents. They'd worked too hard to get to where they were."

"But it wasn't your fault!" said Lupe, raising her voice. "You were raped!"

Elena shot a fearful glance at the nearby tables, but all the other customers appeared engrossed in their own conversations or had their heads buried in their cell phones.

"And Carmen wound up pregnant," I said. "How did she explain that?"

"She put off telling her parents as long as she could. When she finally broke down and told them she was pregnant, they demanded to know the name of the boy. She refused to tell them. They thought she was protecting him. Only I knew the real reason. She couldn't tell them because she didn't know. The father could have been any one of the five boys at the party."

"What about the other girl?" asked Lupe. "Was she also raped?"

Elena snorted again. "At school Monday she accused us of bad manners for ducking out of the party without thanking her for inviting us."

"Did she mention anything about the police?" I asked.

"No, although I think she suspected we'd placed the call. From that day on she never spoke another word to me, but I often caught her giving me the evil eye."

After everything I'd gone through since the death of Dead Louse of a Spouse, I now question everyone's motives. The needle of my Suspicion Meter veered deep into the red zone. "Do you think she set you and Carmen up?"

Elena and Lupe both stared at me. "I...I never considered that," said Elena. "Until about ten years ago."

"What happened ten years ago?" I asked.

"There was that major sex scandal at the school."

"I remember," I said. "A group of seniors competed to see who could have the most sex before graduation."

"Specifically, sex with virgins," said Elena. "They called it 'Cherry Picking' and kept a secret chart listing their conquests."

"Are you suggesting this wasn't a single scandal?" I asked. "That it was a long-standing tradition at the school?"

Elena nodded. "I think I was targeted for a cherry picking that night." Her eyes filled with tears, and she fought to blink them back. "When I asked if I could bring Carmen to the party, I wound up handing her over on a silver platter."

"If that's the case, why didn't previous victims come forward?" I asked. "We've certainly seen that occur in other sex scandals lately."

"Yes, lately," said Elena, "but not ten years ago. Attitudes have changed drastically over the last decade. Besides, most of those other cases involved serial rapists or child molesters, not different groups of boys over many years."

"Did you and Carmen ever discuss the case at the time?" I asked.

She nodded. "The defense argued that not only was the sex consensual, but that their clients were the victims of an orchestrated campaign to score a huge monetary settlement. They painted the rape victims as money-hungry vultures. Is it any wonder no alumni came forward admitting they were also victims in previous years?"

"They'd be accused of jumping on the cash bandwagon," I said.

"Exactly."

Lupe had remained silent, her jaw tightened, while Elena spoke of the sex scandal. When she finally spoke, she practically spit out her words. "Someone has to pay for what happened to you and Mami. What was that girl's name?"

Fear filled Elena's features. Her hands shook. "I...I don't remember."

Lupe leaned halfway across the table. "How can you not remember?"

"It happened half a century ago. No good can come from digging into the past, Lupe. Besides, no one will pay, so what's the point?"

"What do you mean?" asked Lupe.

"Your mother is dead. She can't press charges."

"You can," said Lupe.

"But I won't. I have no proof to back up my accusation."

"What about my mother's baby? Isn't that proof? We could demand DNA tests to find out who the father is."

"No," I said, agreeing with Elena. "First, you don't know how to find your sister. She may not even be alive at this point. And as for DNA tests, even if you could get a court order, a match isn't proof of a rape. The father would claim the sex was consensual, and that he never knew about the pregnancy."

"Besides," said Elena, "do you really think that girl or one of those boys would back up my story after all these years? Why would they? They'd have everything to lose by doing so and absolutely nothing to gain."

Lupe's eyes widened. "You remember their names, don't you?"

Elena rose and forcefully stuffed her arms into her coat. Without making eye contact with either of us, she said, "I need to get back to my mother. She'll be waking from her nap soon and wonder where I've gone." Without saying good-bye, she turned her back on us and strode from the coffee shop.

"How dare she not tell me?" asked Lupe as she stared at Elena's departing back. Her voice trembled, and her eyes filled with tears. Whether from anger or hurt or a combination of both, I wasn't sure.

"She's carried a tremendous amount of guilt for fifty years," I said.

"What do you mean?"

"She feels responsible for what happened to your mother. She brought her to the party."

"All the more reason she should want to help me find the rapist. She owes it to my mother."

"I think she regrets telling you as much as she did, Lupe. We stirred up some long-buried secrets Elena would have preferred stayed buried."

"Then why did she tell us anything?"

"I don't know. I'm not a therapist, but maybe she thought it would bring her some closure after all these years."

Lupe stood and grabbed her coat from the back of her chair. "Well, now I need closure."

I hurried to keep up with her as she stormed out of the coffee shop. "How do you expect to do that?" I asked once we'd arrived back at her car.

"I don't know, but I'll think of something. There has to be a way to find these creeps."

"And then what?"

"I intend to confront them."

I saw this as a really bad idea with no chance of ending well. However, discretion being the better part of valor—or more likely in my case, the coward's way out—I decided against voicing my opinion. I carried my own guilt regarding Carmen. It's why I not only agreed to make the photo albums for Lupe but had accompanied her to meet with Renata this morning. I doubted I'd have the courage to say no if she asked me to help track down her mother's rapist.

~*~

After Lupe dropped me off back home, I bypassed the house and immediately headed to Zack's apartment. "I think she's asking for trouble," I said, after catching him up on the events of the morning. "But how can I dissuade her?"

"If she's determined to follow through with trying to dig up the past, I don't see how you can," he said. "But for her own safety, she should hire a private investigator rather than nosing around herself."

"That's a brilliant idea." Especially if Lupe asked for my sleuthing help. That's when I'd suggest hiring an expert.

"As long as she takes it. And by the way," he added, "I spoke with Patricia. She had the same advice for Cloris and Gregg."

"But the police are already conducting an investigation."

"A PI will dig around in areas where the police might not."

"Wouldn't their attorney have hired one?"

"Maybe. But they might be concentrating their investigation in other areas, at least to start."

"Like what?"

"The buyers' finances, for one, but their motives might be personal rather than financial."

"You mean like they have a vendetta against Cloris and Gregg?"

"Not necessarily. Cloris and Gregg may be victims caught up in a larger scheme. That's why Patricia suggested hiring a PI to follow the couple and dig into their past."

"Hopefully the attorney has already thought of that, but I'll mention it to Cloris."

The morning had drained me. I collapsed onto the sofa. That's when I noticed the packed carry-on bag and camera cases sitting on the floor next to Zack's desk. "Going somewhere?"

He followed my gaze. "I've got some good news and some bad news. Which do you want first?"

"How about if I just take the good news?"

"Sorry. It's a package deal."

I leaned my head back and closed my eyes, hoping that when I opened them, we were in the middle of a different conversation. It didn't work. I sighed. "Where are you off to this time?"

"Back to Madagascar."

"More lemurs?"

"Madagascar Pochards."

"Never heard of them."

"They're the rarest duck in the world and only found in Madagascar. They were thought to be extinct until about eleven years ago when twenty were found at Lake Mastsaborimena. Through breeding programs, the population is now close to a hundred."

"How do you fit in?"

"The ducks are considered critically endangered. I've been hired to take photos for a book and companion calendar that will be sold to raise funds for the conservation program trying to save them from extinction."

"And you just found this out today?"

"It's been in the works for some time, but nothing was firmed up until this morning."

Prior to Zack's last adventure in Madagascar, where he spent two-and-a-half weeks photographing lemurs in the jungle, my only knowledge of the island country had come from the various Dreamworks eponymous animated movies. A quick Google search had informed me of the island's political instability and that travelers should exercise extreme caution.

Zack always seemed to be jetting off at a moment's notice to some area of the globe that scared the caca out of me. He never traveled to Iceland to shoot the Northern Lights or to Italy to document new findings unearthed at Pompeii. His assignments always took him to jungles and deserts rife with drug dealers or terrorists. The skeptic in me wondered if the ducks weren't a cover for a more spy-like assignment from one of the alphabet agencies he swore up and down and seven ways to Sunday that he didn't work for.

Why couldn't he open a photo studio in Westfield and spend his days taking portraits of cute babies? "How long will you be gone this time?"

"Depends on how quickly I capture enough usable images."

Is the Madagascar Pochard a camera-shy duck? "Could you narrow it down a bit? A week? A month?"

"Somewhere in-between."

"And the good news?"

"I finished scanning and touching up the photos we chose for Lupe's albums." He walked over to his desk and retrieved a jump drive, which he handed to me. "All the images are grouped by year and labeled with names and locations I took from the inscriptions on the back of each photo. You can start assembling them whenever you have time."

I stared at the jump drive in my hand, then back up at Zack. A heartfelt *thank you* didn't come remotely close to covering my gratitude. "What did I ever do to deserve you?"

Zack thought for a moment, then shrugged and said, "Maybe it's the universe's way of balancing the scales, given all the crap Karl dumped on you."

I doubted the universe worked on a quid pro quo basis, but Zack had shown up at the lowest point of my life. I don't know if I would have survived this past year without him. "I love you."

"I know."

"When are you leaving?"

"First thing tomorrow morning."

I walked over to the door and flipped the lock. "Then I suppose we'd better make the most of today."

Zack grinned as he took me into his arms. "My thoughts exactly."

NINE

I spent Saturday morning running all those errands single working moms tackle on weekends. Much of that time involved vying for parking spaces and standing in endless cashier lines. Retirees and stay-at-home moms have the luxury of shopping during the week when parking lots are half-empty and cashier lines are short. Not those of us in the workforce. We juggle a week's worth of errands, along with shuttling kids back and forth to various school sports and other extracurricular activities, nonstop throughout our weekends.

At least Alex now had a car, thanks to Ira, which freed up some of my time for yet more chores—specifically housework and laundry. I kept searching for that proverbial light at the end of the tunnel, but I never even caught the briefest of flickers.

Besides, Alex's Jeep arrived with invisible strings, tying us to a quasi-relative who'd wormed his way into our lives. If Ira had never shown up on my doorstep last summer, Mama wouldn't have met Lawrence, and we'd all be better off for that. Except Alex.

Without Ira, he'd still be pedaling around on two wheels instead of driving on four.

I was cooling my impatient Nikes at Shop-Rite, frowning at my cart full of quickly defrosting frozen food, when my cell phone rang. I fished the phone out of my purse and saw Lupe's name filling the screen. "Hi, Lupe."

"I can't find her yearbook," she said in lieu of a greeting, her trembling voice tinged with a combination of depression and anxiety. "I've searched the house from top to bottom."

Nothing like being dropped into the middle of someone else's thought process. "Whose yearbook?"

"Mami's!" Depression and anxiety segued to near hysteria. "I realized last night the yearbook would have a picture of the football team and list everyone's names."

Lupe had lost all sense of logic. I inched up as the first person in line pushed a cart laden with shopping bags toward the exit. The cashier began to ring up the next person in the queue. As sympathetically as I could, I said, "Your mother was a freshman; the boys were seniors. They wouldn't be in her yearbook even if you found it."

"But she should have a yearbook for every year she attended high school, wouldn't she? I did."

"I didn't. Only for my senior year." Yearbooks weren't handed out gratis, at least not in public school. They cost a small fortune. Although anyone could purchase a yearbook, most students waited until their senior year. What was the point of shelling out big bucks for a book filled with upper classman?

"Oh." She sounded like someone had jabbed her with a pin and deflated the balloon keeping all her hopes alive. "I thought everyone did."

"I think it depends on the high school." Both Carmen and Lupe had attended Catholic schools. Maybe their tuition covered an annual yearbook. Even so, Carmen had been shipped off to upstate New York to have her baby. She wasn't attending school in New Jersey the spring of her freshman year. I refrained from mentioning this particular factoid to Lupe, though. It seemed too much like pouring salt into a festering emotional wound.

"The high school!" The air suddenly rushed back into her internal balloon. "Of course! They'd have a copy. She attended Our Lady of Peace. I'll run over during my lunch hour on Monday." With that she hung up, and I inched forward another few millimeters.

~*~

I didn't hear from Lupe again until Monday afternoon. We had just finished up our monthly production meeting, and I was returning to my cubicle when my cell phone rang. Once again, Lupe dispensed with any salutation, jumping right into her reason for calling. "I know who they are!" she said, her voice filled with the sort of excitement I'd expect from someone who had just won the lottery. "I have their names!"

I could barely hear her. Blaring car horns vied with Lupe's voice. "Whose names? Where are you?"

She raised her voice slightly, but I still had difficulty making out her words. "Our Lady of Peace. The library has a collection of yearbooks dating back to the first graduating class in 1927."

"Why is it so noisy?" The Our Lady of Peace complex was situated halfway up the side of a mountain straddling the border separating Watchung and Plainfield. Lupe sounded like she'd hiked down the mountain and was standing in the middle of a mob of angry commuters, all leaning on their horns.

"Sorry," she shouted. "I had the car window down. Better?"

"Somewhat." The cacophony had quelled to a background rumble. "What's going on?"

"Some jerk in a panel van was in too much of a hurry. He nearly ran me off the road in his rush to beat the traffic light. Then he cut off a woman in a minivan. She slammed on her brakes, causing the driver behind her to rear-end her. Now we're all stuck in traffic while the cops sort things out. And of course, the guy who set all of this in motion took off. I hope someone got his license plate number."

"Are you hurt?"

"Not me. The woman in the minivan, and the guy who hit her are being tended to by paramedics, but they look more shaken up than seriously injured. I figured I'd call you while I'm sitting in this mess."

"You mentioned you had names?"

"The football players who raped my mother. I know who they are."

"Players?" Plural? When had Lupe leaped to the conclusion that her mother was the victim of a gang rape? The thought had never occurred to me. Had all the boys at the party taken turns with a comatose Carmen and Elena? I stopped dead in my tracks, my knees growing weak from the sickening thought.

"Anastasia?"

From behind me an arm reached out and grabbed mine, steadying me. I turned sideways to find our editorial director Naomi Dreyfus, a look of concern on her face. "Is everything all right?" she asked.

I hoped so. Surely Lupe's anger over what had happened to her mother years ago—and nothing more—had conjured up the heinous scenario she now suggested. She certainly wouldn't have gained this knowledge from viewing a fifty-year-old high school yearbook. Jocks might like to brag about their conquests, but even the dumbest jock wouldn't mention a gang rape as his most memorable school experience.

"Yes, thank you," I assured Naomi, still conscious of Lupe on the other end of the phone. "I just became queasy all of a sudden." Definitely not a lie.

"Anastasia?" asked Lupe. "What's going on? Are you okay?"

"Yes," I told her. "Hold on a minute."

"I hope it wasn't something in the deli sandwiches," said Naomi.

Naomi always dipped into her petty cash account to provide us with a buffet spread for lunch during our monthly production meetings. Hopefully, the pencil pushers in the accounting department would never catch on. We have few enough job perks at the magazine. I shook my head. "I don't think so. Whatever it was, it's passed now."

"Good. You should sit down, though, just in case." She led me into my cubicle and settled me into my chair. Then she dragged my wastebasket across the floor and positioned it at my feet. "Just in case you can't make it to the restroom in time," she said with a wink.

I nodded my thanks. As soon as she was out of earshot, I returned to Lupe. "How do you know their names?"

Lupe continued to shout into the phone. "I cross-referenced the names listed for the football team with the individual seniors' photos. There were only five seniors on the team that year."

Elena had mentioned there were five boys at the party, all seniors and all on the football team. "What are you planning to do?"

"I'm going to confront each one of them. Four of the five still live in the area."

"How do you know that?"

"I recognized their names. You will, too. If they don't come clean, I'll threaten to go to the press."

That sickening feeling returned to my stomach. "Lupe, you can't resort to blackmail."

"It's the only way I'll get any answers. Trust me, these guys won't want even a whiff of scandal surrounding them, no matter how long ago it happened."

"Lupe, I don't think this is a good idea."

"You're wrong, Anastasia. It's an excellent idea. I need to know the truth, and this is the perfect way to get it." She hesitated for a moment, then asked, "Can I convince you to come with me?"

Absolutely not! As guilty as I felt over Carmen's death, I wasn't about to assuage that guilt by confronting a rapist. I had to stop her. "I understand you need to know what happened, Lupe, but this isn't the way. Zack and I were talking, and he suggested you hire a private detective if you want to pursue this further. Let a professional investigate these men for you."

"Why?"

Lupe was so laser focused on finding her mother's rapist, she didn't realize she might be putting her own life in danger. "It's much safer that way. Please. Think of your family—your husband, your kids. What if one of these guys panics and harms you?"

She didn't speak for a moment, then finally said, "I hadn't thought about that. Do you really think someone would hurt me?"

"I have no idea, but it's certainly a possibility. For all we know, the guy is a serial rapist and has continued assaulting women—or worse—for decades. Who knows what someone like that would do if threatened with exposure?"

Men pushed to their limits often commit acts of desperation. I didn't have to look any further than my own mother's latest husband for confirmation of that. His desperate act had resulted in Carmen paying the ultimate price.

Lupe sighed. "You're right. I suppose I shouldn't rush into a confrontation with anyone just yet."

"Or ever."

"Anyway, I need to do some more research first."

"Internet research?"

"That and going to the library. Elena said she called the police. I want to check the police blotter report in the archives of the local newspaper. I'm hoping they're on microfiche."

"I don't see how that's going to help you. You already know their names. Besides, the newspaper would have protected the boys' identities, especially since Elena claimed charges were never filed against them."

"True, but a report would mention the street where the party was held."

"And then what?"

"That would help me figure out who hosted the party."

"Not necessarily. What if several of the boys lived on the same street? Besides, knowing the host doesn't give you proof of which boy or boys assaulted your mother and Elena."

I heard her mutter something under her breath. "I hadn't thought of that."

She hadn't thought of a lot of things. I feared Lupe would do something rash. "I don't see what you'd gain by spending hours going through a year of newspaper files."

"I can narrow down the timeframe. The rape took place during the school year. I don't suppose you remember Elena mentioning the month, do you?"

I thought about the conversation in the coffee shop. "No, I don't believe she did."

"I'm thinking it must have occurred sometime in the early fall."

"Why?"

"Elena said the family was told Mami won a scholarship to a boarding school for a semester. She probably began showing sometime around Christmas and was whisked off to the nuns for the spring semester."

"I suppose that makes sense." Then I added, "I know I can't stop you, Lupe. Look up the police blotter if you must. Just promise me you'll hire a private investigator instead of contacting these men on your own."

I waited for her response. When she hadn't answered after several seconds, I prodded her. "Lupe?"

She sighed heavily. "All right, I promise."

We said our good-byes, and I disconnected the call. For several minutes I stared at the blinking cursor on my computer screen as I tried to put all thoughts of a five-decades-old rape behind me—not forever but at least for the remainder of the day. Otherwise I'd spend the afternoon consumed with worry for Lupe. I didn't necessarily believe she wouldn't approach those former football players on her own, despite my warnings and her promise.

I shook the stupor from my brain and told myself to get to work. Now that Naomi had signed off on the scrapbooking theme for the next issue of the magazine, I needed to finish Lupe's scrapbook. Because of the condition of the original photos, I needed to factor in the time it would take to publish the albums once I designed the pages and uploaded everything to the online photo service. After the albums were printed and mailed to me, they then had to be photographed for the magazine spread. I also had to write editorial copy for the issue.

In addition, Naomi saw this project as a way to bring aboard a new advertiser. That meant I also had to meet with our sales department to provide them with the information they'd need before they set up a meeting with the online photo service I planned to use.

Designing the pages didn't require much in the way of brainpower, though. The work was intuitive, relying on my innate sense of design. As I worked sizing and arranging the photos on each page in chronological order and by theme, my mind wandered back to the mystery behind Carmen's unfortunate pregnancy.

Ever since Karl's untimely death, I've become obsessed with the butterfly effect. Not how a butterfly flapping its wings in Canada might change weather patterns in Mexico, but how a single act, no matter how small or insignificant, can affect the course of our lives at some point in the future.

I'll never know when Karl began gambling. He kept his addiction well hidden from me. But at some point, either before we met or afterwards, Karl placed his first bet. In doing so, he embarked down an irrevocable path. Was it something as innocent as a frat house poker game? An office Super Bowl pool? A day at the racetrack? Sticking a nickel in the slot of an Atlantic City one-armed bandit? No matter the catalyst, that initial foray into gambling years later changed his life, my life, our kids' lives, and his mother's life forever.

Now Carmen and Elena's innocent act of rebellion fifty years ago, and its devastating aftermath, had set Lupe on a quest for the truth about that night. And I definitely didn't have a good feeling about the flapping of this particular butterfly's wings.

TEN

My phone rang shortly after I arrived home that evening. I hadn't even had a chance to remove my coat and kick off my heels. I fished my cell phone out of my purse and rolled my eyes when I saw Lupe's name on the display. *What now?*

Part of me wished Elena hadn't told us the circumstances surrounding Carmen's pregnancy. I feared Lupe's obsession over finding her mother's rapist might unhinge her, especially if she couldn't find the perpetrator.

Then again, maybe this was Lupe's way of dealing with the grief that consumed her. Focusing on a half-century-old crime might be all that was keeping her from reliving the all too fresh nightmare of a far more heinous one.

Either way, I felt too guilty not to answer her call. I swiped the screen and placed the phone up to my ear. "Hi, Lupe."

"It's Elena," answered a choked voice at the other end.

Calling from Lupe's phone? A cold shiver skittered up my spine. I didn't have to ask to know something was terribly wrong.

"Elena?"

"Lupe's in the hospital."

"What happened?"

"She was crossing the street. A car ran a red light. She's unconscious. The doctors..." She choked on a sob. "...the doctors...they don't know if she's going to make it."

For the second time that day my legs wanted to collapse under me. I grabbed for the wall. "What hospital?"

"Overlook."

"I'm on my way."

I grabbed my wallet from my purse and pulled out a twenty-dollar bill as I headed down the hall in search of my sons. I found them sprawled on their beds, Alex with his nose buried in his chemistry textbook, Nick working on a math assignment.

Alex glanced up as I entered the room. "Hi, Mom. When's dinner?"

I handed him the money. "As soon as you pick it up. Order a pizza. There's salad in the fridge. I need to run out."

"Where?" asked Nick.

"The hospital. Lupe's been injured."

Alex yanked his head up out of his textbook. "How?"

"Hit by a car."

Nick threw his legs over the side of the bed. "Will she be okay?"

I hesitated. Maybe Elena had exaggerated the severity of Lupe's injuries, either due to her own fear or from not completely understanding the doctor. Either way, I thought it best not to say anything to the boys until I had more information. "I hope so."

"If they need someone to watch the kids," said Alex, "we can probably rearrange our schedules." He nodded toward his brother.

"Sure," said Nick. "We'll figure it out."

~*~

Half an hour later I stood outside the ICU, staring at Lupe through a pane of glass. Only immediate family members were allowed inside the room and even then, no more than two at a time.

Bandages wrapped Lupe's head. She wore a full cast on her left leg, which was suspended by a pulley, and another cast on her right wrist. Bruises covered most of her exposed flesh. Andrew Betancourt, Lupe's husband, sat in a chair beside her bed, his hand cupping Lupe's left hand, his gaze fixed on his wife's battered face as he spoke to her. A multitude of tubes ran from her body to an IV and various whirring and beeping machines.

"She's unconscious," said Elena, who had joined me in the hall when I arrived. "The doctors performed surgery to relieve swelling on her brain, but she also sustained internal injuries. They give her about a fifty/fifty chance of making a full recovery. They've done all they can. It's up to Lupe and God now."

"What happened?" I asked.

Elena heaved a ragged sigh. "According to what bystanders told the police, Lupe was crossing Broad Street at Elm, along with several other people. They were all in the crosswalk and had the green light. A panel van came barreling down Broad at a high rate of speed, mowed into them, and kept going. Lupe and two other women took the brunt of the impact. One is in the next room. The other died at the scene."

"A panel van? You're sure?"

"That's what I was told. Why?"

Lupe had nearly been run off Rt. 22 by a speeding panel van earlier in the day. Thousands of panel vans traversed New Jersey roads every day, but could this be more than coincidence? I shook my head. "Nothing."

However, I had an extremely bad feeling about Lupe's accident. Maybe it wasn't an accident. Maybe Lupe's snooping into her mother's past had caught someone's attention, someone who didn't want Lupe exposing his sordid history.

Luckily, Elena didn't press me because I wasn't prepared to explain Lupe's trip to Our Lady of Peace and the earlier near miss on Rt. 22. If I even hinted of a connection between Carmen's rape and the hit-and-run, Elena would blame herself for Lupe's injuries. There was already more than enough guilt going around. I saw no point in heaping on another dose, especially since all I had at this point was conjecture.

I needed to learn if there was a connection between the two incidents. If video existed of the accident on Rt. 22 and the hit-and-run in Westfield, I'd know if the same panel van had caused both. Or perhaps witnesses had taken down the license plate numbers of both vehicles. And I knew just the person to ask, although I doubted he'd divulge any information. He'd parrot the standard line about not being able to discuss an ongoing investigation.

No matter. I simply wanted to plant the seed, alerting Union County Detective Sam Spader of the possible connection between Lupe and the two incidents. Given our history, I was certain he'd find my information credible. And if by chance he didn't? I had more than a passing acquaintance with two of Westfield's finest.

When the P.A. system announced the end of visiting hours, I approached Andrew as he stepped out of Lupe's room. Today's tragedy seemed to have aged him considerably since I last saw him at Carmen's funeral only weeks ago. The fine lines around his mouth and eyes etched deeper into a face once full of life but now old and haggard. Andrew had always reminded me of Mark Ruffalo. Now he looked more like Mark Ruffalo's grandfather.

After telling him how sorry I was, I added, "If you need anyone to watch the kids after school or in the evening, Alex and Nick have volunteered."

He grasped my hands in both of his and fought back tears as he spoke. "Thanks. I think we've got it covered for now with various family members, but I'll keep the boys' offer in mind."

I nodded. He and Elena made their way toward the nurses' station, and I headed for the elevator.

As soon as I returned to my car, I placed a call to Detective Spader. We had met several months ago at the Sunnyside of Westfield Assisted Living and Rehabilitation Center where my mother-in-law was recuperating from a minor stroke. Less than twenty-four hours after Lucille's arrival at the facility, her ninety-eight-year-old roommate was murdered in bed. Based on witness accounts of Lucille's animosity toward her roommate, she became Spader's prime suspect.

I knew my mother-in-law didn't murder Lyndella Wegner. Lucille is all bark and no bite. Mostly. With few exceptions, her loathing of Lyndella was no greater than her hostility toward just about every life form on the planet.

Her dead son and his father top the exceptions list. However, neither thought very highly of her. The former tried to kill her, and the latter walked out on her nearly fifty years ago. The Daughters of the October Revolution might hold her in high esteem as their leader, but not a single member cares enough about her to offer her a place to live, which is why she and I are stuck with each other.

Since I wasn't about to see a killer get away with murder, I had set out to prove Spader wrong. After my nosing around unmasked the true perpetrator, the detective admitted to a grudging respect for me. That respect continued to grow after I helped solve two recent neighborhood murders.

Spader answered his phone on the second ring. This didn't surprise me. From my earlier dealings with him, I suspected he divided the twenty-four hours of any given day between headquarters and his department-issued unmarked car. Perhaps he occasionally crashed in a small apartment somewhere, but judging from his consistently rumpled look, not very often.

The guy didn't appear to have a life beyond his work. He had never mentioned a Mrs. Spader or any little Spaders. I often wondered if his parents were Dashiell Hammett fans, casting their son's destiny when they christened him with a tongue-in-cheek homage to the author's iconic fictional detective.

He answered with his trademark snark. "Mrs. Pollack. To what do I owe this honor? Staying out of trouble, I hope."

I ignored the snark and got straight down to business. "I'm calling about the hit-and-run that occurred in downtown Westfield late this afternoon."

"Why?"

"Have you caught the driver?"

"Not yet. And you should know by now I'm never at liberty to discuss an ongoing case."

I expected nothing less than the standard party line from Spader. "I do."

Annoyance crept into his voice. "Then what's your reason for calling? You have some connection to this case?"

"No direct connection, not with me, but I have reason to believe there may be one between the hit-and-run in Westfield and an accident that occurred earlier in the day on Rt. 22 in Watchung."

"What do you mean?"

I told him about the panel van that had nearly run Lupe off the road hours before the hit-and-run.

"Are you suggesting someone deliberately tried to kill Lupe Betancourt?"

"I'm suggesting you might want to see if the dots connect."

"Are you home?"

"I will be in less than half an hour. I'm leaving the hospital now."

"I'll meet you at your house."

~*~

When I arrived home, I found Detective Spader already waiting for me. As I pulled into my driveway, he cut his engine and stepped from his car. We entered the house together.

"Make yourself comfortable," I said, motioning toward the living room. "I'll be with you in a minute." Spader nodded as he turned into the living room while I went in search of the boys to tell them I was home and report on Lupe's condition.

A moment later I heard Lucille shouting. "How dare you barge into this house? You're trampling on my rights. Where's your warrant?"

I rushed back into the living room. Spader's arms were crossed over his barrel chest, his bushy salt and pepper eyebrows knit together under a deeply furrowed brow. Lucille stood with one hand on her hip, the other clutching her cane. They stood toe-to-toe, glaring at each other. Mephisto cowered under one of the end tables.

Ralph flew in from the kitchen and perched on the bookcase.

"*I throw thy name against the bruising stones,*" he squawked. "*Trampling contemptuously on thy disdain. Two Gentlemen of Verona*. Act One, Scene Two."

Under the circumstances, a rousing chorus of "Hail, Hail, the Gang's All Here" might also have been appropriate, but Ralph only quotes Shakespeare. I stepped between the two warring factions before my mother-in-law provoked Spader enough to cuff her and haul her down to headquarters. It certainly wouldn't be the first time she spent the night in a cell. "I invited him in, Lucille."

She turned on me. "He has no right to search my room."

Spader and I exchanged a knowing glance. The detective was well aware of Lucille's paranoia when it came to the police, but I'm sure he wondered, as did I, just what my mother-in-law had squirreled away in her bedroom. I shook my head, making a mental note to search her room the next time she gallivanted off with her fellow commie sisters. "He's not here about you, Lucille. He has no intention of searching your room."

"Unless I should?" asked Spader, casting a suspicious eye on my mother-in-law.

"Not helping," I muttered under my breath.

Lucille responded by pounding her cane on the floor, a gesture that had little impact, given the muffling properties of the living room carpet, and spearing Spader with her best evil eye. "Unless we're now living in a police state, my privacy is guaranteed by the Constitution." She turned in search of her dog. "Come, Manifesto." Then she waddled out of the living room and down the hall to her bedroom. I don't think she realized Devil Dog had refused to follow her.

Spader stared at Lucille's departing back. "I don't envy you,

Mrs. Pollack."

I matched his frown with one of my own. "*I* don't envy me."

My stomach chose that moment to vocalize—in a less than subtle way—a reminder that I hadn't eaten since lunch. "Would you mind if we speak in the kitchen?" I asked.

Spader chuckled. "Not at all." He followed me through the dining room and into the kitchen. I indicated for him to take a seat at the table.

Alex had said they'd left two slices of pizza for me in the refrigerator, but I discovered the empty box on the kitchen counter. I checked the fridge, hoping to find a plate with the two slices but no such luck. If I had to place a bet, my money would be on Lucille feeding the leftover slices to Devil Dog after the boys cleaned up the dishes. Either that or she returned to the kitchen to scarf them down herself. The woman ate more than the average sumo wrestler.

I settled for a hunk of sharp cheddar, a couple of Granny Smith apples, and a half-empty box of water crackers. I didn't bother slicing the cheese or apples, just placed them on a cutting board with a sharp knife and set them in the center of the table.

A glass of wine would have hit the spot this evening, but I no longer kept any wine in the house. My mother-in-law never met a bottle she didn't consume in one sitting, and I couldn't afford to keep her in the grape. For that reason, all wine was safely locked up in Zack's apartment. Between Lucille's inability to climb the steep staircase outside the garage and her lack of a key, I no longer had to worry about her pilfering my pinot.

I grabbed two glasses from the cabinet and filled them with ice and tap water, placing one in front of Spader, the other across the table from where he sat. Then I added two sets of silverware and plates before settling in the seat across from him. "Help yourself," I said, motioning to the food.

"Thanks. I haven't eaten since lunch." He appeared to have dropped a few pounds since I last saw him, his bulging belly no longer looking nine months pregnant but merely six or seven. I also noticed that the ruptured capillaries on his nose were less pronounced, and his shirt pocket no longer contained the ever-present pack of cigarettes. Perhaps he'd wised up about the precarious state of his health and decided to quit smoking, lose some weight, and cut back on his drinking. If so, he just might live to see retirement, something that was far from a certainty when we first met.

He placed a wedge of cheese on a cracker and popped it into his mouth. Speaking around the food, he asked, "So why am I here, Mrs. Pollack?"

ELEVEN

On my drive back from the hospital in Summit to Westfield I had wrestled with how much to tell Detective Spader. Did I have the right to divulge Lupe's private family history without her consent?

Now as I nibbled on a slice of apple, I finally came to the reluctant conclusion that I had no choice. If today's accidents were somehow connected to Lupe digging into her mother's past, someone was desperate enough to keep her from finding the answers she sought. That person had to be stopped.

I took a deep breath and exhaled the entire story, beginning with Lupe bringing me the suitcase filled with photographs.

"That family has certainly had its share of tragedy," said Spader when I'd finished my tale, "but I'm not sure today's two incidents were anything more than coincidence. I'll have to check with Somerset County to see if they have any information on the driver responsible for the first crash. Did Mrs. Betancourt mention any other details?"

"Like what?"

"Make and model of the vehicle? The color? Condition? Identifying markings? Maybe a partial plate number? Anything that would lead us to connect it to the hit-and-run."

"Nothing, only that it was a panel van."

"Of which there are tens of thousands on the road."

"I know."

"Luckily, we have a detailed description and plate number from the hit-and-run," he said. "If traffic cams caught the earlier incident or the Somerset police have witness reports, we'll know if it's the same vehicle."

"That's what I was hoping you'd say."

He motioned toward the coffee pot sitting on my counter. "Any chance I could bum a cup? I have a feeling it's going to be a long night."

"Of course." I switched on the coffee maker. "Cream? Sugar?"

"Black."

While I prepared the coffee, Spader said, "If anyone else had come to me with this conspiracy theory, I would have dismissed it immediately."

"So, you agree with me that there could be a connection?"

"I think you have a way of seeing things that I've learned to accept as credible."

"Thank you for taking me seriously."

Spader snorted. "Don't let it go to your head. One thing puzzles me, though."

"What's that?"

"You said Mrs. Betancourt discovered the names of the boys who had attended the party by checking a yearbook at Our Lady of Peace. The first accident occurred within minutes of her leaving the school. Given the short timeframe, I don't see how her search

116

to uncover the rapist's name could in any way connect to the crash on Rt. 22."

I'd initially thought the same thing, but I'd also come up with an explanation. "Unless she told someone else about our conversation on Friday with her cousin."

"Did she?"

I placed a cup of steaming coffee in front of him. "I don't know. She never mentioned speaking with anyone else, but that doesn't mean she didn't." And if she did, perhaps that person told others. Dozens of people might now know that Lupe was investigating what had happened to her mother as a young teen, and one of them might have a reason for silencing her.

Spader scrubbed at the stubble covering his jaw, his mouth set in a deep grimace. "If she did tell someone, that person's name is trapped inside the brain of a woman in a deep coma."

He leaned back in his chair and nursed his coffee, his expression thoughtful. Finally, he said, "Those former football players would have the most to lose if one of them found out Mrs. Betancourt was digging up old secrets. I don't suppose you have their names."

I shook my head. "It shouldn't be hard to figure out who they are, though. Lupe said there were only five seniors on the team that year. She also mentioned I'd recognize some of their names."

Spader placed his drained cup on the table and stood. "I'll look into it. Maybe we'll get lucky and discover one of them owns a panel van with front-end damage."

"Is it ever that easy?" I asked as I walked him to the door.

He snorted. "In all my years on the job? Occasionally a perp is so stupid that the case pretty much solves itself, but it doesn't happen very often. The worst are the cold cases, the ones that never get solved. There are far too many of them."

That last thought darkened his expression. Spader was a good cop who didn't like to lose. One unsolved case was one too many. I knew he wouldn't rest until he found the guy who'd run down Lupe and the two other women. He reached for the doorknob.

Before stepping outside, he turned to me and said, "Do me a favor, Mrs. Pollack."

"Sure."

"Stay out of trouble."

And here I thought he was about to ask for my help. I tamped down the urge to reply with a salute and an "aye, aye."

~*~

Detective Spader called the next afternoon. "Looks like there's no connection between the two incidents yesterday. A navy panel van caused the accident on Rt. 22. The hit-and-run in Westfield involved a white panel van."

"What about the football players?" I asked.

"We did a little behind-the-scenes investigating so as not to tip our hand, just in case your theory had some serious teeth."

"Did it?"

"Turns out four of the guys had alibis for yesterday during the two incidents."

"And the fifth?"

"He died less than a year after he graduated high school."

"How?"

"Drug overdose."

Had he turned to drugs to deal with a guilty conscience? Then again, if you believed the books, movies, and music that came out of the sixties, a huge number of teens and young adults took part in the drug culture back then. "None of the four own a panel van?"

"Negative. We found the vans abandoned. Both had previously been reported stolen."

"Were they discovered near each other?"

"Miles apart. The blue van was found parked next to a vacant warehouse in Secaucus. The white van was abandoned behind the Walmart in Union."

"What about fingerprints?"

"Wiped clean."

"Are car thieves usually that smart?"

"The ones who don't want to get caught are."

"So you have no clue as to who mowed down Lupe and the other two women?"

"It's early in the investigation, but with the involvement of two separate vehicles, it seems obvious there's no connection between the two incidents."

"Which means you believe the person responsible for the hit-and-run didn't deliberately try to kill Lupe?"

I heard Spader heave a deep sigh before he answered. "All I can say at this point, Mrs. Pollack, is that I don't see how the hit-and-run connects to a fifty-year-old rape. That doesn't mean the driver wasn't bent on harming Lupe for some other reason or had targeted one of the other two women. We just don't know yet. However, in my experience these cases are rarely premeditated."

"Meaning?"

"The driver is usually intoxicated or on his phone and not paying attention. Once he hits someone, he panics and takes off, especially if he's driving a stolen vehicle. Most likely Mrs. Betancourt and the others were just in the wrong place at the wrong time yesterday."

Maybe. Or maybe not. My guilt over Carmen's death had now

led to Lupe's injuries. And what if Lupe didn't survive? I owed it to her to dig a little deeper. Perhaps Spader and his fellow detectives had overlooked something. "I don't suppose you'd be willing to share the names of the former football players with me, would you?"

"Not a chance, Mrs. Pollack. You keep your nose clean on this one. Let us do the work we're trained to do."

"But you have no leads."

"I never said we have no leads; I said the members of the football team aren't suspects in the hit-and-run."

"But—"

"We'll catch the creep."

"How?"

Annoyance seeped into his reply. "I don't have time for this, Mrs. Pollack. I've already wasted too many hours on a dead end." With that he hung up.

I buried my head in my hands. Spader's confidence that he'd crack the case did little to assure me. After all, the man had sat at my kitchen table last night, bemoaning numerous unsolved crimes. What made him so certain he'd solve this one?

"You okay?"

I turned to find Cloris, a bakery box in her hands, standing in the entrance to my cubicle. I shook my head. "Not really."

She flipped open the lid to reveal half a dozen iced brownies. "Everything is always better with chocolate and booze."

I helped myself to one of the brownies. "Booze?"

"Remember that gourmet bakery that made adult-only cupcakes infused with liqueurs?"

"How could I forget hundred-proof cupcakes?"

"They've expanded their repertoire to include brownies."

120

I took a bite. A marriage of chocolate and Chambord exploded on my taste buds. "Tell me we don't have to share these with anyone else."

"Share what?" Cloris winked. She closed the box and placed it on my counter. "I'm going to the break room to grab coffee for us. Don't scarf down all of these while I'm gone. I've got dibs on half of them."

She returned a minute later with two steaming cups of coffee. After grabbing a brownie and taking a bite, she settled into the spare chair in my cubicle and asked, "What's going on?"

Cloris had been out of the office all morning. I hadn't had a chance to tell her about Patricia's suggestion that she and Gregg hire a private investigator or about the hit-and-run. I started with the easier news—the information that affected her.

"One thing I've learned about high-priced attorneys," she said, "they keep PI's on retainer. Someone is already snooping around the trolls. Hopefully he'll find something incriminating, but that can't be why you look like someone pulled the feathers off your parrot. What's going on?"

I inhaled a deep breath of courage before telling her about the hit-and-run.

She nearly choked on a mouthful of brownie. "My God! Will Lupe survive?"

"I don't know, but even if she does, she may have extensive brain damage. And it's all my fault."

Cloris gaped at me, her jaw hanging open, her eyes bugging out. "Wait! I'm confused. Were you the driver?"

"Of course not! How could you think such a thing?"

"Maybe because you said it's your fault? How the heck are you responsible for Lupe's injuries?"

"It all started with Cynthia's death. If I had accepted the initial police report, Lawrence wouldn't have orchestrated the murders on my street to keep me from discovering the truth. Carmen would still be alive. Which means Lupe wouldn't have found the suitcase of photographs, and I wouldn't have discovered the letter about Carmen's secret baby."

"Whoa! What secret baby?"

Cloris had been so wrapped up in her own problems that I realized I had never told her about the suitcase of photos and all that had transpired after I found the letter addressed to Lupe. I quickly caught her up.

"Don't you see, Elena telling us about the rape set Lupe off on a quest to discover her mother's rapist." I took a deep breath. "I set the first domino in motion. None of the other events would have taken place otherwise."

Cloris rolled her eyes. "And if Fidel Castro had been a better baseball player, the Yankees would have signed him, and there never would have been a Cuban Revolution, the Bay of Pigs, or the Cuban Missile Crisis. And maybe JFK wouldn't have been assassinated."

I reached for another brownie. "I hate to break it to you, but that story about Castro and the Yankees is a myth. Good try, though."

"So how about this: if Gregg and I had turned down that offer on our house and sold to some other couple, we wouldn't now be dealing with a spurious lawsuit."

I stared at her over the rim of my coffee cup. "Your point?"

"You can't live your life second-guessing every decision you make. It serves no purpose other than to drive you crazy."

"Welcome to Team Zack. He keeps trying to tell me the same

thing."

"Smart guy. You should listen to him. Besides," she continued, "didn't you say your detective friend found no connection between the rape suspects and the hit-and-run?"

"He said they all had alibis for yesterday. There's a difference." If I'd learned one thing from living my entire life in New Jersey, it's that for the right price alibis are always for sale. Just ask any member of organized crime.

"Why do I get the sneaking suspicion you're planning an investigation of your own?"

Was I? I suppose the idea had lurked in the back of my mind from the beginning, even though I'd claimed I didn't want to get involved in Lupe's family drama. However, that was before she wound up in a coma. Now I owed it to her to find her mother's rapist. "Maybe the hit-and-run has nothing to do with a decades' old sexual assault, but someone has to uncover the truth."

"Seems to me I also remember you saying the detective told you to leave the detecting to him."

"Of the hit-and-run. Not the rape."

"Okay, Sherlock, let's say you discover who raped Carmen. Then what?"

What, indeed? Wasn't that the question I'd posed to Lupe? And hadn't Elena and I explained to her the futility of pursuing the truth? But Lupe had insisted she needed closure. At least if I uncovered the identity of the rapist, I could provide her with that—if she ever woke up.

~*~

On my way home from work I stopped at the hospital to see if Lupe's condition had improved. Elena and I met at the entrance to the hospital. A late November wind whipped around us as I asked, "How is she?"

Elena hugged her arms around her body and shook her head. "No improvement so far."

I shook my head in sympathy. "I'm so sorry." Then I added, "I'm glad I ran into you, Elena. I need to speak with you about something."

Her eyes grew wary. "Yes?"

Initially I hadn't wanted to tell Elena about Lupe's trip to Our Lady of Peace. I didn't want her blaming herself for Lupe's injuries. That was yesterday. Today everything had changed. I inhaled an icy breath of courage, then on a rush of air told her Lupe had discovered the names of the football players hours before the hit-and-run. "I think someone may have targeted Lupe."

Even if Spader saw no connection, one still might exist. Getting Elena to cough up those names would save me countless hours of searching, especially since I'd ruled out my own visit to Our Lady of Peace to check the yearbook.

Although remote, the possibility existed of a link between the school and the driver of the blue panel van. I needed to employ extreme stealth sleuthing to remain totally anonymous throughout any investigating I undertook.

Elena's response shocked me. Her eyes narrowed, and she spoke through gritted teeth. "Stay out of this, Anastasia."

I took a step back. "But—"

"I never should have told you and Lupe anything about that night."

"I need those names, Elena."

"What difference could knowing the names possibly make now?"

"Lupe needs closure."

"Closure? She's in a coma."

"When she comes out of the coma."

"Forget it. You won't get those names from me."

"Why not? Think of Lupe."

"I am thinking of her. Now if you'll excuse me, I have to get home to fix dinner for my mother." She pushed me aside and hurried toward the parking garage.

I stared after her. Elena's hostile attitude told me my theory wasn't so far-fetched. No matter what Spader believed, I was now convinced someone had tried to stop Lupe from uncovering the truth. Elena was spooked. If I found the person she feared, I'd find the rapist.

I entered the hospital and made my way up to the intensive care unit. Andrew once again sat beside his comatose wife, his hands cupping one of hers as he spoke to her. He looked even worse than he had last night. I doubt he'd slept. He certainly hadn't shaved.

I stood on the other side of the glass, waiting for him to notice me. When he finally glanced my way, he rose and met me in the hallway.

"It's so good of you to come again, Anastasia. I've told Lupe you came last night. The doctors said I should talk to her as much as possible. It might help her come out of the coma."

"I've heard that."

He sighed. "I have no idea whether or not she can really hear me. Part of me thinks it's a myth."

"A myth?"

"One the hospital staff perpetrates to keep family members occupied and feeling useful." He shrugged. Tears filled his eyes.

"Who knows? If there's the remotest possibility of it helping, I'll talk until I lose my voice."

"Andrew, did Lupe mention anything about the two of us visiting Elena last Friday?"

He nodded. "She told me what she learned about her mother, if that's what you mean."

"Did you know she wanted to hunt down the men involved?"

He ran both hands through his already unruly hair. "I tried to talk her out of it."

"As did I, but she didn't listen to either of us."

"What do you mean?"

"You didn't tell anyone about what happened to Carmen and Elena, did you?"

"Of course not. What's this all about?"

"Lupe discovered the football players' names shortly before the hit-and-run."

The color drained from Andrew's face. "You don't think someone deliberately tried to kill her, do you?"

"I don't know. I talked to one of the detectives on the case. He thinks it's a coincidence."

"What if it's not?"

"Exactly."

"Do you know the names?"

"I don't, and both the detective and Elena refuse to divulge them to me."

"I can understand the detective not sharing but Elena?"

"She's afraid of something. Or someone."

"What do you need from me?"

"I suspect Lupe wrote down the names."

"Her purse and clothes are still here. I've been hoping she'd wake up soon, and I'd be able to bring her home. Wait here."

Andrew stepped back into Lupe's room. I watched from the other side of the glass as he pulled her purse from the closet. He returned to where I waited and together we looked through it but found nothing.

"What about her phone?" I asked. "Does she take notes on it?"

He fished her phone from the side pocket of her purse, turned it on, and tapped on the Notes app. "Nothing," he said, scrolling down the titles of the various notes Lupe had made.

I thought of one last place we could search. "Pockets?"

Andrew returned to the room. A moment later I saw him pull a folded piece of paper from Lupe's coat pocket. He opened it and stared at the page. The color drained from his face.

TWELVE

Andrew returned to the hallway and with a shaking hand, passed me the creased sheet of paper, a photocopy of a yearbook page. A large picture of the entire football team filled the top half of the page. Below that were five small individual photos of the senior members of the team. I read each of the names and recognized four of them. I now knew why both Detective Spader and Elena had refused to share the names with me and why Andrew now looked like a sickly ghost.

"These have to be the boys from the party," I said. "According to Elena, the five boys at the party were all seniors and all football players."

Andrew turned his head to focus on his wife as he spoke. "Four of them are very powerful, well respected men."

I studied the photos of the boys posing in their football uniforms. "With an enormous skeleton in each of their closets."

Peter Donatello was a high-powered defense attorney who practiced in New York and New Jersey. He specialized in white-collar crime and had amassed an extremely high acquittal rate throughout his long career. Could he be the rapist? Had he orchestrated the hit-and-run? A man with crooks for clients had certain connections, but Peter Donatello only handled insider trading and embezzlement cases, not mob-related crimes where someone might know a guy who knew a guy who could make a problem disappear without leaving a trace.

Albert Owens had inherited his slumlord father's real estate empire back in the nineties. First, he kicked out the welfare tenants, druggies, and squatters. Then he tore down the rat-infested, dilapidated buildings. In their place he erected million-dollar high-rise condos along the Jersey side of the Hudson River, transforming worn down, blue-collar neighborhoods and slums into a gentrified urban paradise with spectacular views of the Manhattan skyline.

Being in construction, Owens probably knew guys who knew guys, but he'd always maintained a squeaky-clean reputation. Would a man like that hire a hit man?

Mickey Rigato was a state assemblyman from Union County. He'd been in New Jersey politics for decades and had a reputation for getting things done—for the right price, if you believed the rumors. Then again, pay-to-play had always gone hand-in-hand with New Jersey politics. Knowing how to work the political system for your constituents didn't mean you'd go to extreme lengths to cover up an old crime.

Quarterback Rodney Renquist had spent his entire adult life in football, playing first at Rutgers University, then several years for the New York Jets and Miami Dolphins before injuries forced him off the gridiron and into a career as a college coach back at Rutgers. He had established a charitable foundation that raised millions of dollars in scholarship money for inner-city kids. Everything I knew about the man placed him firmly in the "good guy" category. Was he making amends for a crime he committed half a century ago? If so, I didn't see him compounding that crime by going after Lupe.

The fifth boy, Kirk Zysmerski, was apparently the one who died of a drug overdose shortly after graduating. I returned to my earlier thought when Detective Spader first told me of the overdose. Given the decade in which Zysmerski died, had he over-indulged in recreational drugs or had his drug use resulted from a need to deaden the memory of a certain event in which he'd taken part? Unfortunately, the answer would remain buried with the deceased.

"These men couldn't possibly be responsible for what happened to Lupe, could they?" asked Andrew.

"Probably not, but I'd like to be absolutely certain, wouldn't you?"

He turned back toward me and nodded. "Of course, and I'm sure if there is a connection, the police will find it."

I hoped so. Whoever ran down Lupe and those other two women deserved to go to prison for the rest of his life.

Detective Spader claimed the four men all had alibis for the time of the hit-and-run. However, powerful men have ways of creating an impenetrable wall between them and their criminal acts. They rarely commit any physical crime themselves, instead relying on others to do their dirty work for them. By throwing enough money at the right person, a powerful man with connections (and what powerful man is without connections?) can buy his way out of any situation, no matter how compromising or criminal.

All of these men had much to lose from even a whiff of scandal. An accusation of rape stunk far greater than a mere whiff, even if the crime had occurred half a century ago.

Had one of them gone to extremes to keep the story firmly buried in the past? And if so, how had he discovered Lupe was investigating what had happened to her mother and Elena that night?

I pondered these questions as I drove home from the hospital. When Elena sat down with Lupe and me at the coffee house on Friday, she claimed she'd remained silent about the rape for the last fifty years. Given her refusal to divulge the names of the boys at the party, I was quite certain she hadn't spoken to anyone else after she left us, especially since she now regretted telling us what had happened to her and Carmen that night.

Lupe had told Andrew, but he swore he hadn't mentioned the incident to anyone. Had Lupe spoken to someone else besides her husband and me? Perhaps someone at Our Lady of Peace? Surely Lupe wouldn't have been foolish enough to divulge her reason for wanting to view the yearbook. Or had her rage so consumed her that she lost all common sense and spit out accusations the moment she saw the yearbook photos?

Even though all four men had alibis for yesterday afternoon, one of them might have a relationship with someone who worked at the school, someone Lupe spoke with or who had overheard a conversation she had with someone else. If Lupe had mentioned the rape, that person might have placed a phone call afterwards—a phone call that led directly to the hit-and-run.

I certainly wasn't about to go snooping around the school asking questions of someone who might have a connection to a rapist/murderer. Still, with Spader refusing to draw a line leading from the rape to the hit-and-run, I owed it to Lupe to make absolutely certain—beyond the smallest iota of doubt—that the two incidents were absolutely, positively, in no way on God's green earth, connected. If I didn't, my guilt would prevent me from getting a decent night's sleep for the remainder of my life.

What I needed was a credible way to question a coach, a real estate developer, an attorney, and a state assemblyman without raising any suspicions or tipping off the wrong person. And even if I did come up with a way to speak with each of them, how could I steer the conversation to a party that had taken place fifty years ago that would connect one of them to yesterday's hit-and-run without putting my own life in jeopardy?

That question plagued me throughout the night. Sometimes when I'm trying to solve a problem, the answer will often come to me in the middle of the night as I'm trying to fall asleep or while I'm in the shower. I've often used my finger to scrawl my thoughts on a steam-covered glass shower enclosure before I forget them. And I always keep a pad and paper on my bedside table because if I don't immediately write down the answer that comes to me, it's gone in the morning. I might remember I solved a problem the night before, but in dawn's early light, that solution evaporates like an elusive dream.

~*~

Unfortunately, no such solution presented itself to me throughout the long sleepless night or while I showered the next morning. The pad beside my bed lay open to a pristine white page; no brilliant idea marred the steamy glass as a steady stream of hot water pounded my groggy body. I left for work tired, grumpy, and thoroughly annoyed by my lack of success.

When I arrived at work, I headed directly to the break room

for a much-needed infusion of caffeine and a sugar rush. Cloris took one look at me, and asked, "What's with the scowl? This morning's selection of pastries not to your liking?"

"Huh?"

"You've been frowning at that box of mini croissants for a full minute. Either you can't make up your mind between chocolate raspberry and almond peach, or you don't care for either choice, which I seriously doubt. I've known you too long."

I glanced at Cloris, then at the empty plate in my hand. Had I really been staring at the bakery box for an extended period of time? Or had I fallen asleep on my feet? Anything was possible.

I shook away the massive cobweb that had a stranglehold on my brain and filled a plate with one of each flavor. "It's not the croissants. They look delicious."

Cloris refilled her coffee cup and poured one for me. She then helped herself to a chocolate raspberry croissant. "Missing Zack?"

I added cream to my coffee before downing half the cup in one long swig. "Without question but that's not my problem this morning."

"Then what? I can't figure out if you're sleep deprived or angry over something. Or perhaps you're angry over being sleep-deprived?"

"All of the above."

"Spill."

I glanced down at the half-cup of coffee in my hand. What was she talking about? I hadn't spilled anything. Then I realized she'd spoken figuratively, not literally. Boy, was I out of it this morning!

As we headed to our cubicles, I caught Cloris up on the events that had transpired since we'd last spoken of Lupe. "I need to figure out a way to talk to these guys to prove whether or not one of them had anything to do with the hit-and-run."

Cloris followed me into my cubicle and settled into my spare chair. I collapsed into my desk chair.

After popping the remainder of her chocolate raspberry croissant into her mouth, Cloris pointed to my computer screen. "The answer is staring you in the face, Sherlock."

I turned to look at the screen, which displayed one of the layout pages for Lupe's photo album. Great. I didn't even remember stopping in my cubicle and turning on my computer this morning before heading to the break room, but I must have. I looked down and realized I wasn't wearing my coat. I spied it hanging on the hook beside the entrance to my cubicle. Had I been sleepwalking? I turned back to Cloris. "How do you figure?"

She sighed. "You need to go home and get some sleep because the Anastasia Pollack I know would have figured this out immediately."

I took a bite of croissant and washed it down with a swig of coffee before speaking. "Okay, we've established I'm not operating on all cylinders this morning. So how about if you state the obvious solution that I'm obviously missing."

"Why not interview them for your photo album article for the magazine?"

"And ask them what? Did you rape a classmate fifty years ago and try to kill her daughter the other day?"

"I'd be a bit more subtle."

"You think?" However, her suggestion began to sound less absurd the more I mulled her words around in my foggy brain.

"These men will be celebrating their fiftieth class reunion this year. I could approach the interviews from that perspective, tying them into the importance of preserving family memories for their children, grandchildren, and generations to come."

"Exactly. You're a crafts editor, not an investigative reporter. This wouldn't be a hardball interrogation that might raise suspicions, but you can pepper the interview with a few questions about regrets and youthful indiscretions, gauging their reactions."

Cloris was an absolute genius. "Because sometimes body language and what's left unsaid speaks volumes more than actual words. This could work."

"You'll have to interview more than the four men you suspect of the rape."

"Of course."

"Make the group a cross-section of seniors in their late sixties and older—white color, blue color, men, women. Perhaps set up the interviews to speak with husbands and wives together since it's the wives who usually take care of preserving family photos and memorabilia."

"Good idea."

"And see if Naomi will allow you to take along our staff photographer. People love getting their picture in a national magazine, especially politicians."

She held my gaze for a moment, her underlying subtext written across her face. The staff photographer shot my craft spreads in our studio on the first floor or on location shoots, but unless we needed a professional portrait for a celebrity, I'd always handled any shots of guest crafters and other mere mortals on my own. I didn't need our six-foot-three burly photographer for his skills with a camera. I needed him for his muscle in case one of my subjects saw through me. "I doubt Naomi will agree to that."

Cloris shrugged. "You never know unless you ask."

The photographer notwithstanding, Cloris's suggestion had

perked me up like a shot of triple-strength espresso. I raised my coffee cup in a mock salute. "I'm in your debt."

"Yes, you are." She stood and took a bow. As she departed my cubicle, she stopped, glanced back over her shoulder, and offered me a catbird grin. "And you're welcome."

Once I finished my coffee, I made my way to Naomi's office, only to meet up with her halfway down the corridor. Kim O'Hara, Naomi's fifty-percent Irish, fifty-percent Chinese, one hundred-percent efficient assistant, followed at her heels. "Got a moment?" I asked, stopping in front of them.

Naomi glanced over at Kim. "How's our time?"

Kim glanced down at her phone. "You're three minutes early."

Turning back to me, Naomi said, "I'm on my way to a meeting upstairs, but I can spare a minute or two."

I quickly explained Cloris's ingenious idea for expanding the craft spread on scrapbooking to include interviewing various seniors. Naomi struck a thoughtful pose, her index finger pressing against her chin as she mulled over my suggestion. "Yes, I like this idea."

She turned back to Kim. "Make a note that we need to pull two additional editorial pages from one of the other sections for Anastasia."

I held a virtual breath as I asked one more question. "Would it be okay if I take the staff photographer with me on the interviews?"

Naomi raised an eyebrow. "Why?"

"To get some shots of the interviewees."

"But why do you need a photographer?"

I didn't. "Some of the people I have in mind to interview are local celebrities of a sort."

She practically snorted. "Of a sort. But you're not interviewing Hollywood prima donnas with demanding publicists. You're more than capable of shooting a few candid photos of your subjects, Anastasia. You've done so countless times in the past. We don't need to increase your budget for the issue to have the photographer accompany you."

I had expected her answer. I was on my own with no backup muscle to protect me if I wanted to question these guys. I'd better not screw up.

I spent a huge chunk of the remainder of my workday on the phone, setting up interviews. At first, I thought I'd have a tough time getting the four men to agree to sit down with me, given who they were and the fact that I worked for a third-rate women's magazine sold at supermarket checkout counters. I'd even devised a list of bullet points to employ if I needed to do a bit of verbal cajoling. To my surprise, though, none of them needed their egos stroked. All immediately agreed, eager for the national publicity.

Vanity, thy name is over-the-hill male baby boomers.

The hard part over, I lined up a few additional people to interview by contacting several seniors I'd met when I moonlighted last summer as the arts and crafts teacher at the Sunnyside of Westfield Assisted Living and Rehabilitation Center.

Fame is addictive, no matter how late in life it comes. Having already experienced a bit of celebrity from taking part in a recently published issue, the Sunnyside men and women were more than eager for an additional opportunity to extend their newfound status as kings and queens of their particular fiefdom.

Now all I needed to do was come up with a list of questions that might wheedle some useful information out of my four prime suspects without raising their suspicions.

I'd scheduled two of the men's interviews for the next day and two for Friday, wanting to get them done as soon as possible before I lost my nerve. I would have preferred tackling them all in one day, but the distance between locations prevented so tight a schedule. I left the stress-free Sunnyside residents' interviews for early next week.

Every time my phone rang throughout the day, I sent up two silent prayers: one, that Lupe had come out of the coma and showed no lasting complications and two, that Detective Spader had caught the hit-and-run creep and found absolutely no connection to any of the four men. I received seven calls but only two on my cell phone, both wrong numbers.

By quitting time each of my two prayers remained unanswered, but at least I ended the day having finally devised a series of non-confrontational, lightweight questions for the interviews. Would they work? I wouldn't know until I asked them.

Of course, since I'd become the universe's favorite punching bag, I wasn't surprised to find myself stalled between exits in yet another traffic jam on Rt. 78. I grabbed my phone and sent Alex a text: Traffic mess on 78. ETA unknown. Dinner in fridge. Don't wait.

He replied a few seconds later: Will wait. Text when ur off 78.

As I sat and sat and sat, only inching a few feet forward every ten minutes or so, a cold rain began to fall. Every so often my headlights picked up a snowflake mixed in with the icy raindrops. I flicked on my wipers and cranked up the heat.

I could have passed the time listening to music, meditating, or playing brain games to help ward off dementia in my old age.

Instead, this worrywart spent the next ninety minutes imagining all that could go wrong during my interviews tomorrow. By the time I arrived back in Westfield, I'd woven myself into a complete basket case.

Then I turned into my driveway and burst into tears.

THIRTEEN

I've never been one to wax poetic over an automobile. I don't understand the all-consuming passion men have for horsepower-filled shiny metal boxes. As far as I'm concerned, all a car needs is safety and reliability. However, seeing the silver Boxster parked in my driveway filled me with uncontrollable emotion.

Zack was back, signaling that all would eventually be right with my world. Plus, given the darkened apartment above my garage and my kitchen ablaze with lights, odds pointed to dinner waiting for me. I turned off the engine, wiped away my tears, and raced from my car through the icy rain to my back door.

He greeted me with a smile that silently announced he had missed me as much as I had missed him. I flew into his arms, unconcerned that my mother-in-law sat in full view of my passionate welcome home kiss. If we'd been alone, I'd have given him quite a bit more. Right there in the kitchen.

"About time you decided to grace us with your presence," said Lucille. "Do you have any idea what time it is, Anastasia? I shouldn't have to wait halfway to bedtime for dinner. But then again, thoughtfulness isn't a trait with which you have even a passing acquaintance, is it?"

I breathed in the garlicky aroma of sautéing seafood, a far cry from the turkey burgers and string beans Lucille would have had to settle for had I arrived home on time, and bit back the comment sitting on the tip of my tongue. Instead, I chose to ignore her. No way would I let that acerbic communist curmudgeon spoil the mood for me.

"The ducks cooperated?" I asked Zack, my arms still encircling his neck.

"Not a camera-shy one among them. Turns out Madagascar Pochards are aware of their circumstances and want off the critically endangered list. You'd think they'd seen *Sunset Boulevard* because they immediately harnessed their inner Norma Desmond."

"Ready, willing, and able for their close-ups?"

"Without a doubt. I have it on good authority the Ford Modeling Agency is preparing contracts as we speak."

"Today a calendar and book deal, tomorrow the cover of *Vogue*?"

He winked. "Anything's possible. They are rather photogenic."

Lucille expressed her annoyance over our banter by exhaling one of her classic *harrumphs*. I glanced over at her and found myself the recipient of a dagger-filled glare. I turned back to Zack. "I suppose we should serve dinner."

"Preferably sometime this century," said Lucille.

~*~

Since Alex and Nick would like nothing better than for Zack and me to marry, they eagerly offered to clean up the kitchen after dinner. "You two probably have a lot to talk about," said Alex as he cleared plates from the table.

"Among other things," whispered Nick, loud enough for Zack and me to hear.

I fought to keep a straight face as I issued a parental admonishment. "No TV or video games until you've finished your homework."

Nick saluted.

"Wouldn't think of it," said Alex. Luckily, I knew he meant it. Given my financial situation and with college looming on the horizon, he needed to keep pulling down straight A's if he had any chance of securing a scholarship.

Once Zack and I entered his apartment, he grabbed a bottle of wine from the refrigerator and poured two glasses. A sauvignon blanc would have been the perfect accompaniment to our seafood dinner but thanks to my mother-in-law, we had to settle for an after-dinner glass well out of her sight.

Zack handed me one of the glasses, and we got comfortable on the sofa. "Did you finish Lupe's photo album while I was gone?"

"Not quite. Something happened." I choked back the lump forming in my throat. "Lupe's in the hospital. In a coma."

"Jeez! What happened?"

I told him about the hit-and-run. "There's an outside possibility it was deliberate."

"Road rage?"

I shook my head. "More like she was targeted."

"Why?"

I drained my wine glass, then from the beginning, explaining how Lupe had discovered the names of the boys at the party the night Carmen and Elena were raped and how after her visit to Our Lady of Peace, she was nearly run off the road. "I called Detective Spader and told him of my suspicions. He didn't find a connection between the earlier incident and the hit-and-run. He also checked into the whereabouts of the four men that day and said all have solid alibis. He's convinced it's nothing more than coincidence."

"But you don't?"

I shook my head. "I'm not sure. I need more proof."

"Why do you think Lupe was targeted?"

"Gut instinct? Maybe one of those men put out a hit on her." These things happened all the time, often for nothing more than one punk feeling another punk had disrespected him. "After all, this is New Jersey. Hiring a hit man is often as easy as ordering a pizza."

Zack knit his brows together and shook his head. "That quickly? I think you're letting your imagination run away with you."

I sighed. "Maybe. But I have to know for certain. Given everything that's happened, it's the least I can do for Lupe."

"What do you mean?"

"This is all my fault."

"Here we go again. For the hundredth time, none of this is your fault."

"It is. When I questioned Cynthia's death, I set all these events in motion. Carmen would still be alive, and Lupe would never know about her sister or the rape. The hit-and-run may be just a tragic accident. Or maybe not. But if I can find out who was responsible for what happened to Carmen—"

"Hold on!" Zack grabbed me by the shoulders, shaking me slightly. "You're not planning to confront these men, are you?"

I inhaled a deep breath before answering him. "Confront is an extremely strong word."

"Give me a better one."

I explained about the interviews I'd arranged.

He jumped to his feet, raised his arms, then slapped them against his thighs. "That is the absolute worst idea I've ever heard."

I shrugged. "It's the best I could come up with."

He dropped back down onto the sofa. "You really think one of those men will admit what happened that night? No one would be that foolish."

"Probably not, but you never know what someone will say in an interview, especially if they remember the evening as just a wild party that occurred during the freewheeling sixties. After all, neither Carmen nor Elena ever pressed charges. Those men may not believe they did anything wrong."

Zack didn't say anything, just stared at me as the seconds ticked away. Finally, he raked his hands through his hair and said, "It's a good thing those ducks cooperated. I'm back from Madagascar in the nick of time."

"For what?"

"I'm taking on a pro bono assignment."

"For whom?"

"For you, sweetheart. I know I can't talk you out of this harebrained idea. So, I'm tagging along to these interviews as your photographer-slash-bodyguard. Hopefully, you'll only need me for my prowess with a camera."

As opposed to...what? His fists? Or worse yet, his gun? Maybe this whole interview scheme of mine wasn't such a brilliant idea after all.

FOURTEEN

The next morning Zack and I set out to meet Coach Renquist and his wife at their home in the quaint, historic village of Cranbury, New Jersey, one of the many Washington-slept-here towns that dotted the state. An overcast sky threatened snow, even though the weather report had predicted nothing more than an occasional flurry. I placed my non-existent money on the ominous gathering clouds, not the overpaid, surgically enhanced meteorologist on the morning news. She obviously hadn't bothered to look out her studio window before stepping in front of the cameras.

Because Rutgers had lost their final game of the season on Thanksgiving Day, with Michigan State knocking them out of playoff contention, the coach had plenty of time for a non-football interview. His wife, he'd told me on the phone, loved to make scrapbooks and even had a dedicated craft room in their home.

The Renquists lived in a modest white clapboard Victorian one block off the village's North Main Street shopping district. They answered the doorbell together.

As a couple, the Renquists were polar opposites in looks. The coach, towering well over six feet, had retained much of the muscular physique of his playing days, except for the slightest of paunches straining the knit of his red Scarlet Knights sweater. He wore his steel gray hair in a modified marine buzz cut that should have created a no-nonsense air about him, but a perpetual twinkle in his eyes offset the sternness of the flattop.

In contrast, Mrs. Renquist was a petite dumpling of a woman whose head barely reached up to her husband's shoulder. Her rosy cheeks and wire-rimmed glasses reminded me of Mrs. Claus—the one from the North Pole—if Mrs. Claus paid for expensive salon highlights and dressed in Lilly Pulitzer.

After introductions the couple ushered us into a cozy front parlor filled with overstuffed Ethan Allen furniture. Several needlepoint pillows, including a few with the Rutgers emblem and mascot, decorated the sofas and chairs. A blazing fire crackled in the fireplace, the mantle lined with trophies from the coach's playing days. A tea service and platter of homemade cookies sat on the coffee table, which was situated between the two facing sofas.

"Please, sit," said Mrs. Renquist. She motioned toward the table as Zack and I made our way to one sofa while she and the coach settled into the other one.

"I took the liberty of preparing some refreshments," she continued as she lifted the teapot. "How do you take your tea, Mrs. Pollack?"

"With lemon," I said. "And please, call me Anastasia."

"Then you must call me Bernadette." With a pair of silver tongs she dropped a small wedge of lemon into the tea, then handed me the delicate floral patterned porcelain cup and saucer that so perfectly matched the décor of the room.

"I feel I already know you," she continued. "I've read your magazine for years and have made many of the craft projects you've featured."

"I'd love to see some of them."

Her face lit up. "Would you, really?"

"Of course. As well as your scrapbooks. Your husband tells me you're an avid scrapbooker."

"Yes, Rodney said you wanted to discuss scrapbooking."

"The feature I'm writing is about the importance of preserving and handing down family memories."

The coach patted Bernadette's chubby thigh. "My wife has certainly done that."

"I'm in the process of creating an album for the daughter of a neighbor who recently passed away," I said. "The daughter stumbled upon a suitcase of old photos in her mother's attic. That's what gave me the idea for the magazine feature."

The coach motioned to the built-in bookcases that flanked either side of the fireplace. "Bernadette's been making scrapbooks since we first met. We have shelves of them."

"And when did you meet?" I asked as I retrieved a tape recorder from my purse. I held it up and asked, "Do you mind? It's easier than scribbling notes."

"Not at all," he said. "We met in kindergarten."

My eyebrows shot up to my hairline. "You've been scrapbooking since you were five years old?"

Bernadette laughed. "Not exactly. Rodney exaggerates. I always saved mementos, though. By the time I was in my twenties, I had amassed dozens of shoeboxes filled with photographs, greeting cards, ticket stubs, concert programs, anything that connected to a special memory."

"She even kept the wrapper from the first candy bar I shared with her," said the coach. "A Three Musketeers bar."

Bernadette blushed. "It's true. I eventually preserved the contents of all the shoeboxes in scrapbooks."

"We both knew from the day we met that we were meant for each other," said the coach.

His wife nodded. "It was love at first sight. For both of us. We married the day after we graduated college. Neither one of us ever dated anyone else."

Zack was busy taking candid photos as they spoke. I briefly caught his eye and saw that the same thought had entered his mind at the moment it entered mine. Rodney Renquist may never have dated anyone else—that his wife knew of—but that probably hadn't kept him from having sex with another woman. Or two.

"No one?" I asked.

"Never," they both replied in unison, smiling at each other as they clasped hands.

I wanted to believe them. They came across as the poster couple for happily-ever-after. Maybe the coach left the party before Carmen and Elena passed out, but why was he even at the party that night without Bernadette? By their own admission the two were attached at the hip from Day One.

As I continued to chat with the couple, I realized I really wanted to eliminate Coach Renquist as a suspect. However, I saw no way of directing the conversation to the circumstances surrounding that infamous night without admitting my ulterior motive for being in their home. Any suggestion of wrongdoing on his part would destroy a lifetime of love Bernadette had for her husband. How could I plant suspicions about him in her mind?

"You two seem to have led a charmed life," I said. "Any regrets?

Anything you wish you could go back and say to your teenage selves?"

An expression of puzzlement settled across Bernadette's face, as if the concept of regret seemed foreign to her. "What do you mean?"

I shrugged nonchalantly. "Perhaps a warning not to do something you did back when you were a teenager or advice about doing something differently?"

Bernadette grew thoughtful. Finally, she said, "I did always regret not taking a fourth year of French in high school."

Coach Renquist laughed. "Well, I certainly have one huge regret."

"What's that?" I asked.

"I'd have run the ball myself instead of passing to Pete Donatello in the fourth quarter the last game of our senior year. He fumbled the ball. Trinity Catholic retrieved it and went on to score the winning touchdown. We were undefeated for the season until that game."

"And he's never let Pete forget it," said Bernadette.

"You still keep in touch with your former high school teammates after all these years?" I asked.

"Of course, as well as my college and pro teammates. Football is a brotherhood, much like the armed services. We're bonded for life."

Great! It had never occurred to me that the senior football players from Our Lady of Peace continued to maintain their friendship over the past half century. Women often sustained lifelong friendships from childhood through their twilight years, but I'd never known a man to do so. Men didn't bond the way women did, at least not in my experience.

I had scheduled an interview with Peter Donatello for later that afternoon. I wondered how often my four interviewees spoke with one another. Was it no more than the exchanging of Christmas cards and a phone call once a year, or did they get together once a week for beers and poker?

What if one of them mentioned their sit-down with me, and they compared notes? They'd never believe I randomly selected the four of them out of a state population of over nine million. I darted a quick glance toward Zack. He didn't say a word, but his expression told me he was thinking the same thing. If one of the four had put out a hit on Lupe, my goose was cooked—to a crisp.

I fought to keep the worry out of my voice or from showing on my face and pressed on with the interview. "High school, college, and the NFL? That's a lot of players. You keep in touch with every single one of them?"

"All who are still living." He grew somber for a moment. "We've lost a few good men over the years. Cancer. Heart attacks. One died in a car accident." He paused for a brief moment. "And a few other tragedies that never should have happened."

Bernadette and the coach turned to face each other, sorrow written in their expressions. She squeezed his hand; he squeezed hers back.

I assumed he referred to Kirk Zysmerski's drug overdose, but since I wasn't supposed to know about that, I quickly changed the subject. "You have a fifty-year high school reunion coming up, don't you? Are you planning to attend?"

"Wouldn't miss it," he said, turning back to me. "Of course, I would have liked to attend with a national college championship trophy to show off after all these years. Never did land one of those for my coaching."

"There's always next year," said Zack.

The coach shook his head. "Now that the season's over, I'm hanging up my cleats for good."

"Retiring?" I asked.

"It's time. We bought a Winnebago and plan to travel around the country while we're still young enough and in good health."

"Sounds like a great way to enjoy retirement," I said. "I'm assuming it goes without saying, that football is your fondest high school memory?"

"Football and Bernadette."

I chuckled. "Very diplomatic of you, Coach."

We chatted for a few more minutes while we finished our tea. Then Bernadette removed the tea tray from the table and replaced it with half a dozen of her numerous scrapbooks. The first two scrapbooks covered the couple's early childhoods, one book for Bernadette, one for the coach.

"No siblings?" I asked Coach Renquist, noting the absence of other children in the family photos as Bernadette highlighted various pages.

He shook his head. "Not for want of trying. My mother suffered a series of miscarriages both before and after my birth. Eventually, my folks gave up trying, grateful for the one healthy kid they had."

If nothing else, with no younger sister, that eliminated the coach as the host of the party Elena and Carmen had attended.

After flipping through each page and describing the events surrounding many of the photographs and mementos, the coach occasionally adding side commentary, Bernadette replaced the books on the shelf and pulled out the next half dozen. This went on for two hours until we'd covered the length of their decade's long relationship, ending with the recent birth of their seventh grandchild.

When Bernadette finished showing off her scrapbooks, we were given a tour of the house. In each room she proudly pointed out the crafts she'd created. Zack continued taking candid shots throughout the tour. We ended in Bernadette's craft room where she showed me a variety of projects in various stages of completion.

Three hours after we'd arrived, we said our goodbyes to the couple. A light dusting of snow now covered all non-paved surfaces. Wind-whipped flakes swirled around us as we hurried down the street to Zack's Boxster. "So, what does your sixth sense tell you?" he asked once we'd settled into his car and he turned over the engine.

I chewed on my lower lip. "I don't know what to think." As we drove out of Cranbury toward Princeton, the location of my second scheduled interview, I thought about the time we'd spent chatting with Coach Renquist and his wife. I saw no telltale signs to suggest the man was hiding a horrible incident from his past and nothing to indicate Bernadette knew anything about that infamous night. "The two of them come across as a loving, open book."

Of course, I'd lobbed only softball questions at them. "Unless Coach Renquist is one of the greatest actors of all time, he certainly doesn't strike me as someone who would have taken part in drugging a couple of innocent girls and raping them, let alone trying to cover up his involvement years later by hiring someone to run down Lupe."

"Could Elena be mistaken about the number of boys who attended the party? Maybe the coach wasn't there."

I watched the windshield wipers swish back and forth several times before I responded. "I'd like to believe that."

Zack remained silent until we stopped at a local diner for lunch. After we placed our orders, I studied his face. His expression told me something else weighed on his mind, probably the fact that the four guys kept in touch and how I may have put myself in danger—yet again. As much as I hated the anticipated conversation, I needed to let him vent his concern. "I see brain gears spinning."

He grimaced, then reached across the table to take hold of my hands. "I don't want you to think I'm making light of what happened to Carmen and Elena, but perhaps we should consider other possibilities."

Definitely not the opening I expected. "Meaning?"

He paused while the waitress returned with our coffees, then inhaled a deep breath before he continued. "Suppose Elena's memory of what happened at the party isn't quite accurate."

"What memory? She doesn't remember anything that happened to her and Carmen. She was drugged."

"I'm sure she believes that."

I stared at Zack, watching dumbfounded as he poured cream into his coffee, then gave it a stir. "Are you suggesting what I think you're suggesting? That the rape never occurred? How is that possible? Carmen wound up pregnant."

"I don't doubt that. However, the circumstances surrounding the pregnancy might not be exactly as Elena described them."

"Zack, you weren't at the coffee shop when she confessed to Lupe and me. The woman silently carried that disturbing secret around with her for fifty years. Those memories are real. I'm sure of it."

"I'm not suggesting Elena lied to you and Lupe. She may believe every word of what she told you."

"Then what are you saying?"

"Just that sometimes our brains protect us from that which we'd rather not remember by planting false memories to replace actual ones."

"So she made up the story about a rape? What could possibly be worse than what she told us?"

"Guilt of some sort?"

"Over what?"

He shrugged. "I don't know. It's only a theory."

"But why would Elena make up such a horrible story?"

He took a sip of coffee. "Maybe it has nothing to do with guilt and everything to do with Elena's need to play the victim. Look what you recently uncovered about Betty Bentworth."

While investigating Betty Bentworth's untimely demise, I'd learned she'd suffered from Munchhausen by Proxy. Prior to moving into the house across the street from me, she'd spent decades in prison for poisoning her children. Luckily, she hadn't succeeded in killing them.

Maybe Zack was on to something, especially given Elena's reluctance to talk further about that night and the other people involved. If so, all four men might be totally innocent, and the hit-and-run was just a tragic accident with no connection to Carmen's past.

The waitress returned with our orders—a club sandwich for Zack, a Cobb salad for me. After she refilled our coffee cups and departed Zack continued playing Devil's Advocate. "And consider this—what if there was no party?"

"Elena claimed after she and Carmen left the house, she called the police to report underage drinking."

"But you only have her word. You don't know if the police received a call that night. Even if they did, one of the neighbors might have placed the call. Elena may have learned of the party and the boys being hauled off to the station after the fact when she went to school the following Monday."

I thought back to the letter we found, the letter that set so many recent events in motion. "Carmen's letter to Lupe talked of her own guilt and a mistake *she'd* made, not a horrible crime committed against her."

"Exactly."

"But rape victims often believe they're at fault, even nowadays." I'd watched enough episodes of *Law & Order: SVU* over the years to know that much. "Carmen's pregnancy occurred half a century ago. Her guilt may have come from blaming herself for leading on one of those boys."

"Or guilt over sleeping with her boyfriend."

That had been my initial thought until Elena wove her tale of rape. Having died, Carmen was in no position to refute Elena's story.

"We also should consider Elena's mental state," said Zack. "What do you know about her?"

"Next to nothing."

"She may have a history of fabricating stories."

If she did, I had no way of finding out, not with Lupe in a coma. Certainly, none of her relatives would share such sensitive information with me. Besides, if Lupe knew Elena was a pathological liar, she would have questioned everything Elena told us.

This certainly put a new spin on events. I'd have to wait to see if we discovered any relevant information during the remaining three interviews.

FIFTEEN

Peter Donatello had scheduled a fifteen-minute interview with me. "That's all his schedule will allow," his secretary had informed me. "He's booked solid."

Under the circumstances, I wondered why he'd agreed to see me at all. I suspected free publicity in a national magazine tipped the scales in my favor. After all, you never know when some housewife who grabs a copy of *American Woman* while standing in line at the supermarket might need a white-collar criminal defense attorney.

The offices of the Donatello Law Group took up the entire fifth floor of one of the office buildings in the Carnegie Center, a massive office park complex on Rt. 1 in Princeton. Over the years the firm had represented many a state assemblyman or senator caught accepting a bribe or dallying in other questionable behavior that compromised both their office and the public's trust. Given the state of New Jersey state politics, the Donatello Law Group never lacked for clients.

After giving our names to the receptionist, Zack and I took seats in a waiting area to the right of the reception desk. If I didn't know better, I'd think we had entered an exclusive men's club. Dark hand-rubbed mahogany wainscoting covered the lower half of the walls with the upper half papered in a navy, gold, and burgundy plaid. A thick Persian carpet in matching shades filled most of the solid wood flooring that designated the waiting area. Burgundy-colored leather wingback chairs, separated by leather-topped cherry end tables, each holding a brass lamp, lined the two adjacent walls. At any moment I expected a butler to appear with a tray holding snifters of hundred-year-old brandy and a box of Cuban cigars.

Twenty minutes after our scheduled appointment time a curvaceous twenty-something wearing a cleavage-exposing black knit dress arrived to escort us to Peter Donatello's office. Following several steps behind her, I caught a glimpse of the trademark red soles of her Christian Louboutin ebony suede stilettos as they clicked along the polished wood floors. If secretaries now made salaries that enabled them to purchase thousand-dollar designer shoes, I seriously needed to consider a career move. "Mr. Barnes and Mrs. Pollack," she said after opening the office door. She stepped back to allow us to enter, closing the door behind us.

Peter Donatello rose from behind a massive antique carved desk that I suspect cost more than my house. As we made our way across a luxurious jewel-toned Bokhara rug, Zack held back, allowing me to precede him by a few steps as we approached the other side of the desk.

The former high school wide receiver wore a pinstriped charcoal suit, which screamed bespoke from the perfect way it fit his body. He glanced back at Zack, frowned slightly, then extended his hand toward me. "Mrs. Pollack."

He wore an enormous onyx-framed, square-cut diamond and gold pinkie ring that twinkled in the light from overhead recessed cams. Matching diamonds of equal size glittered from his starched white shirt cuffs. I reached across the desk to meet him halfway and received a bone-crushing handshake that caused me to bite back a wince. He held my gaze for a moment before releasing my hand. Classic testosterone move, I thought. Male domination rearing its chauvinistic head.

Donatello then offered his hand to Zack. "You look familiar," he said. "Have we met?"

"I don't believe so."

"I never forget a face."

"Nor I, and I'm certain I would have remembered yours."

Oh goody. Two alpha males vying for top dog position. "Perhaps you both attended the same charity event at some point," I said. "The Met Gala, maybe?"

Donatello's eyebrows rose. "You've been to the Met Gala?"

"Most years," said Zack. "Have you?"

Donatello ignored the question, his lips forming into a tight line, his silence suggesting he'd never received an invitation to the prestigious event. Instead he nodded to the two chairs in front of his desk. "Please, have a seat. How may I be of service?"

"Won't Mrs. Donatello be joining us?" I asked.

His expression grew puzzled. "Why on earth would you want my wife here?"

I explained the thrust of my article. His puzzlement quickly segued into annoyance. "I thought you were here for a legal consultation."

Now I was puzzled. I studied the man seated across from me, a man whose wealth emanated from the top of his perfectly styled full head of thick silver hair to the gold Rolex on his wrist to his expertly manicured fingertips. "I explained my reason for wanting the interview to your secretary. She said you'd be delighted to take part."

He huffed out his displeasure. "My longtime secretary retired recently. The new girl obviously didn't inform me of the nature of this appointment. If she had, I wouldn't have agreed to it."

"I see."

He rose from his chair. "This is a well-respected firm, Mrs. Pollack. I'm not some cheap ambulance chaser who advertises on cable networks. Why on earth would I jeopardize my firm's standing by granting a frivolous interview to some insipid women's magazine? You've wasted your time."

He didn't even bother to apologize for the misunderstanding. Instead he pressed a button on a console on his desk. When his secretary responded, he said, "Brittany, please escort Mr. Barnes and Mrs. Pollack out. Then get back in here right away."

"Yes, Peter."

Peter? Rather informal for a recent hire.

A moment later Brittany appeared at the door. Zack and I took our leave of Peter Donatello's office, following Brittany's sashaying booty and clicking designer footwear back to the reception area.

"Arrogant, smug misogynist," I muttered under my breath as we waited for the elevator. "I can't believe he and Coach Renquist were ever friends, let alone that they still spend time together. Those two are polar opposites."

Zack chuckled. "He really got to you, didn't he?"

"Did it show?"

Zack replied by laughing again.

"You think he's getting it on with Brittany?"

"I seriously doubt he hired her for her secretarial skills," said Zack.

"Well, as far as I'm concerned, if there was a rape, he's now at the top of my suspects list. And I wouldn't put it past a man like that to have friends in low places who are willing to do his bidding for the right amount of money."

"Lots of men are scumbags," said Zack. "Few are rapists and murderers."

"Granted, but all rapists and murderers fall firmly into scumbag territory."

~*~

Since I had scheduled the remaining two interviews for the following day, Zack and I returned home. He had a date with his Madagascar Pochards—or at least their photographic images— and I needed to finish work on Lupe's album.

With the day half-over and the weather growing worse, I saw no point in heading to the office. Instead, I decided to spend the remainder of the day working from home. At least that was the plan until Zack turned onto our street, and we spied a Westfield patrol car idling at the curb in front of my house.

In front of the patrol car sat Harriet Kleinhample's rusty circa 1960's orange Volkswagen minibus, its wheels straddling the curb. As was often the case with the way Harriet parked, the Volkswagen's front bumper rested against the trunk of my oak tree. I feared one of these days the tree would decide it had had enough of the abusive relationship and would fight back, crushing the minibus under its massive trunk.

"What now?" I cursed under my breath as Zack pulled into the driveway. Officers Harley and Fogarty stood at my front door. Fogarty, the taller and younger of the two by a head and a decade, pounded his fist against the door while his pudgy partner Harley shouted a demand to open the door.

The pounding and shouting ceased when the two cops noticed our approach. "Boy, are we glad to see you, Mrs. Pollack," said Harley.

"What's going on?" asked Zack.

"Another hit-and-run downtown," said Fogarty.

SIXTEEN

It took a moment for Fogarty's words to sink in. *Another* hit-and-run? What the heck was going on in Westfield lately? "Was anyone hurt?"

"Luckily, not this time," said Harley. "One vehicle struck another."

I hold a Bachelor's Degree in art, not criminal justice, so I don't claim to know all the ins and outs of investigative procedure. However, I failed to see how this latest incident connected in any way, shape, or form to the previous one that had killed one woman, seriously injured another, and left Lupe in a coma. "Why are you here?" I asked Harley and Fogarty.

"The traffic cam captured an old orange VW minibus speeding through the red light," said Fogarty. "It clipped the front end of the car that had the right-of-way and kept going." He nodded toward Harriet's rusty orange relic. "The license plate wasn't visible in the video, but you don't see many of those old VW minibuses still on the road."

"Except for the one that's often parked in front of your house," said Harley. "The minibus has front-end damage consistent with the accident, but your mother-in-law refuses to open the door."

"Does that surprise you?" I asked.

"Hardly." He scowled at the door. On the other side we could hear a cacophony of communist magpies.

Due to my mother-in-law's anarchistic disregard for the law, Harley, Fogarty, and I had more than a passing acquaintance. Lucille's behavior often resulted in her receiving overnight accommodations at the Westfield hoosegow. The town's entire force understood the cross I bore.

Sometimes I think they locked her up for a minor offense just to provide me with a few hours' respite. However, they'd never admit to that, lest word got out and other town residents demanded equal treatment under the law. Turns out I'm not the only Westfield resident burdened with a cantankerous in-law.

Harley and Fogarty had also come to my rescue on more than one occasion, including a series of break-ins last winter. As a result, no matter how little money I had, I didn't begrudge a single tax dollar that went toward Westfield's finest.

I withdrew my house key from my purse and unlocked the door. When it swung open, we found Lucille standing on the other side, feet spread, one arm planted on a hip, the other gripping her cane, a tight-lipped scowl firmly in place. A gaggle of gray-haired Daughters of the October Revolution stood behind her.

"Get out!" shouted Lucille. "You have no right to enter this house."

I stepped in front of the officers. "I invited them in."

She glared at me. "I should have known you'd have something

to do with this."

"In case you've forgotten, you're a guest in my home, not the other way around."

"You'd never get away with this if my son were still alive."

A constant Lucille refrain, second verse same as the first. "I'm a law-abiding citizen helping the police solve a crime."

"It wasn't her fault," said Lucille.

"What wasn't her fault?" asked Harley. "Running the red light, hitting another vehicle, or leaving the scene of an accident?"

"All of it," said my mother-in-law.

"She can tell it to the judge," said Fogarty. "Step aside."

Lucille refused to budge.

Harley turned to me. "Which one owns the vehicle?"

I pointed to Harriet Kleinhample, dwarfed behind my mother-in-law's massive body. Harriet could pass as Estelle Getty's doppelganger, but unlike the star of the old *Golden Girls* sitcom, Harriet possessed a mean streak second only to my mother-in-law.

"You're not taking her," said Lucille. She raised her cane menacingly close to Fogarty's head. With her other hand she shoved him with all her might, but she was no match for the amateur bodybuilder. He neither flinched nor budged—until in a swift blur he whipped out his handcuffs and slapped them on her.

A moment later both Lucille and Harriet, cuffed by Harley, were marched out to the patrol car. The other women followed, screaming about police brutality. Fogarty stopped and turned to face them. "Would you ladies like to join your friends in lock-up tonight?"

That shut them up. After Lucille and Harriet were placed in the back seat of the squad car, Harley nodded toward the minibus and said, "We'll send a tow truck to impound the vehicle."

"You can't do that!" said one of the women.

"How will we get home?" asked another.

Harley shrugged. "Not our problem, ladies."

"Call an Uber," said Fogarty. Then taking mental count of their number, added, "Better make that several Ubers."

He slid behind the steering wheel of the patrol car. As Harley settled into the passenger seat, Fogarty stuck his head out the window and asked, "You posting her bail this evening, Mrs. Pollack?"

I glanced into the back seat where my mother-in-law sat seething and muttering. When she noticed me looking at her, she speared me with an evil eye that needed no interpretation. I shook my head. Lucille didn't suffer from dementia or diminished mental capacity of any sort that might excuse her behavior. She was just a nasty old commie who didn't care about anyone other than herself, her dog, and her fellow Sisters of the October Revolution. I turned back to Fogarty. "I'm done. She's on her own."

"I warned her," I told Zack as the squad car pulled away from the curb and drove down the street. We'd been down this road too many times before. Every time I posted Lucille's bail, I worried that she'd skip town, and I'd wind up even more in debt. The last time she'd gotten herself arrested, I'd issued an ultimatum. If she couldn't post her own bail this evening, she could sit in a cell until she came before the judge on assault charges.

Zack wrapped his arm around my shoulders. "You deserve a medal for exercising such superhuman patience with her."

"Part of me hopes the judge throws the book at her. I can use the vacation." I twisted my neck so our eyes met. "Does that make me a bad person?"

"I'm not blaming you."

I nodded toward the group of women glaring at us. "They do."

"Do you care?"

"No, but I suppose we should drive all of them home."

Zack and I studied the group of women, coatless and huddled together for warmth against the snow. Flakes gathered on their eyelashes before melting into large droplets that streamed down their cheeks. As the wind whipped around us, several glanced back toward the house where they'd left their outerwear. Others wrapped their arms around their torsos and stamped their feet.

"There are too many of them to fit into your car and mine in a single trip," said Zack. "And I'm guessing you don't want to leave any of them alone in the house while we shuttle the others."

"Definitely not." Who knew what revenge these women would take against me for allowing the police to cart off Lucille and Harriet?

Zack pulled his phone from his pocket. "It's too cold to leave them waiting on the sidewalk. Fogarty had the right idea. I'll order up a few Ubers."

I ushered the women back into the house to wait for their rides. I was about to offer them cups of hot tea and coffee to warm themselves when I noticed they'd helped themselves to lunch. Dirty dishes covered my dining room table. I entered the kitchen and found open containers of food lining the counter. Someone had spilled milk on the counter and hadn't bothered to wipe up the mess. Mephisto slurped at the puddle that had collected on the floor.

The sight before me released my inner bitch. Once more I cursed under my breath as tears filled my eyes. With my precarious financial situation, I couldn't afford to waste food. I'd had enough of these selfish, ungrateful women and their leader. If I had to, I'd padlock the refrigerator and the pantry, leaving only enough food available each day for Lucille's lunch. Nothing more.

"No way am I offering those commie octogenarians hot beverages while they wait," I told Zack as he helped me return whatever food remained to the refrigerator and pantry. I then stood in front of the open refrigerator and surveyed the depleted contents. The Daughters of the October Revolution had helped themselves to the food I'd planned to serve for dinner that night.

"We'll order takeout," said Zack.

I glanced at the clock on the stove, worried my sons would be driving home from school in what was quickly becoming a major storm. But at that moment I heard Alex's car pull into the driveway. I sighed with relief. One less worry. "The snow is getting worse. Will anyone deliver in this weather?"

"You're forgetting something," said Zack.

"What's that?"

"Neither snow nor rain nor heat nor gloom of night stays the pizza deliveryman from the swift completion of his appointed rounds."

"And here I always thought that was the mailmen's creed."

"Mailmen and pizza deliverymen."

~*~

An hour later Zack, Alex, Nick, and I were finishing up our pizza dinner. The thieving commies had bypassed the refrigerator salad crisper during their food raid, leaving me the fixings for a healthy accompaniment to an otherwise carb-and-calorie-loaded dinner. The pizza even arrived semi-hot. A few minutes in the oven brought it back to optimal temperature. Zack and I even enjoyed a glass of wine with dinner, thanks to Lucille's absence.

The boys were clearing the dishes and loading the dishwasher, and Zack was feeding a bit of pizza crust to Ralph when the phone rang. I glanced at the caller ID, noted Cloris's name on the display, and answered the call.

"You're not going to believe this," she said.

"What?"

"We received a threatening letter from The Sentinel."

"What did it say?"

"He called us liars for denying we'd received that previous letter from him and said we'd be sorry."

Something didn't sound right. I mulled over Cloris's words for a moment before it hit me. "How would he know you denied having received the letter? Did you refute the buyers' claim to anyone other than me?"

"Only the police and our attorney. I'm assuming our attorney told their attorney."

"And no one mentioned it to any reporters?"

"We haven't spoken to any reporters. Neither has our attorney. And nothing about our denial appeared in any of the news articles I've seen about the lawsuit."

Neither had anything turned up in my online searches. The lawsuit only stated that the buyers claimed The Sentinel had contacted Cloris and Gregg several days before settlement.

I also knew from my prior interactions with the police that no one on either the town or county force would divulge such information. They'd mouth the standard line about an ongoing investigation. "So how would The Sentinel know you deny having received correspondence from him?"

Silence hung on the line between us. Finally, Cloris said,

"Damn, you're good. Ever consider leaving the magazine business and hanging out a shingle?"

"Hardly. I'm not that good. I merely employed simple deductive reasoning. If you weren't so tied up in knots about this lawsuit, you would have come to the same conclusion immediately. Anyway, I think you've got them. There is no Sentinel, Cloris. You and Gregg are the victims of a couple of con artists."

"How do we prove that?"

"You don't. Leave it in the hands of the police and the detective your attorney hired. This note is the buyers' first slip up. It won't be their last. Guaranteed."

"I hope you're right. I haven't slept in days." A yawn punctuated her words.

After we ended the conversation, I filled Zack in on what Cloris had said while we took Mephisto out to do his nightly business. Three inches of snow covered the driveway and sidewalk. Large flakes continued to fall, whipping around in the wind. Another few miles per hour, and we'd reach full-fledged blizzard mode.

Mephisto is not one of those dogs that loves to romp in the snow. Zack had to drag him to the nearest tree, the one Harriet Kleinhample had dinged yet again earlier in the day.

"I agree with you regarding the scam theory," he said as we waited for Mephisto to sniff out his target. "Nothing else makes sense at this point."

"Unless The Sentinel is omnipotent," I said, stamping my feet to keep warm.

Zack raised an eyebrow. "Highly unlikely."

Well, duh!

Mephisto finally christened the tree and surrounding snow, then made a beeline back toward the house, dragging Zack with him. I'd never seen Devil Dog run so fast. I guess he didn't like cold paws—or cold anything else. Which begs the question: if dogs are so smart, why haven't they learned to use litter pans?

~*~

The storm petered out by nine o'clock that evening. We woke the next morning to a winter wonderland certain to devolve into a gray slushy mess within hours. For now, though, I enjoyed the pristine sparkling beauty of the undisturbed snow as I sipped my morning coffee. With my first interview not scheduled until ten-thirty and my mother-in-law still the unwilling guest of the Westfield police, I took pleasure in a long steamy shower and a leisurely morning breakfast, compliments of the amateur chef who had shared my bed last night.

"Where to this morning?" asked Zack as he flipped pancakes.

"Albert Owens and his wife. We're meeting them at their home in Bedminster."

Owens had retired and turned his business over to his two sons. He and his wife divided their time between their New Jersey estate and a semi-private island in the Bahamas. They'd flown his private jet back to New Jersey to host their annual extended family Thanksgiving Day bash. I'd caught them days before they were scheduled to fly back south for the winter.

"Does he know why you want to interview him?" asked Zack.

"His secretary passed along my request."

Zack placed a plate of pancakes, sausage, and eggs in front of me. "I hope she does a better job of relaying messages than Brittany."

"No need to worry. Mrs. Owens returned my call to schedule

the appointment. We had a nice preliminary chat on the phone. I got the feeling she'd like to hire me to organize her photos. She said she has decades of photos stored in dozens of plastic shoe boxes on her closet shelf."

"Would you?"

"Certainly." Even though my debt rivaled the GNP of Djibouti, Mrs. Owens probably spent more on yearly salaries for her household staff. I'd be delighted to organize her family snapshots in return for a sizeable check. Then again, billionaires are often notorious skinflints. "Depending on what she's willing to pay."

~*~

A locked gate separated the Owens estate from the surrounding Bedminster countryside. Zack pressed the button on a console situated on the side of the short driveway leading to the gate. A voice on the other end asked us to identify ourselves. When Zack gave our names, the gate swung open, allowing us to proceed up an already plowed and salted, tree-lined, winding road. The estate, hidden from the main road and large enough to double as a boutique hotel or a small castle, came into view as we made the last turn.

I gaped at the sprawling faux French chateau, easily twenty thousand square feet in size, which placed it at least fifteen times larger than my own home. "I'll bet there are rooms in that house no one ever enters except for the maids when they dust. Why does anyone need such a huge home?"

"Status," said Zack.

"I could live like a queen on what they probably pay in real estate taxes every year."

"Jealous?"

I shrugged. "Not really. However, if Virginia Owens does want me to organize her family photos, she's going to pay enough for me to cover my real estate taxes for the year."

Zack barked out a hearty laugh as he parked the car on the circular drive in front of the house. He continued chuckling under his breath as we ascended the brick stairs that led to the home's double-door entrance. "What's so funny?" I asked.

He waved his arm to indicate the house and surrounding estate. "You really expect me to believe you're not the least bit jealous of all this?"

Busted. "I suppose if I had a house this large, I could assign Lucille to her own wing, provide her with a personal maid, and never have to deal with her."

He laughed again. "Now you're talking."

Once he regained his composure, I rang the doorbell. The door swung open before the chimes pealed the seventh note of Beethoven's "Ode to Joy." A woman dressed in full servant regalia, complete with white starched apron over a utilitarian black dress, stood before us. She even wore one of those frilly white maid's caps I've never seen anywhere other than in old black and white movies and PBS dramas.

When I introduced myself, she ushered us into a white marble foyer as large as my living room, dining room, and kitchen combined. A sweeping marble staircase curved around the back half of the room from the left side, winding its way up to a second-floor balcony. A massive crystal chandelier suspended over the center of the foyer caught the sunlight streaming in from floor-to-ceiling windows. Hundreds of rainbows produced by the chandelier's prisms, danced along the circular foyer walls.

After taking our coats, the maid led us into a sitting room to the right of the foyer and said, "Wait here, please. Mrs. Owens will be with you shortly."

I tried not to gawk at my surroundings, filled with antique furnishings and several original Impressionist paintings hanging on the walls. Not just any Impressionists, either. I counted two Renoirs, a Degas, and a Monet.

Before Dead Louse of a Spouse had slipped his earthly coil and left me in debt up the wazoo, we had lived a comfortable middle-class life, even though in my blissful ignorance I had no idea we lived a smoke and mirrors existence built on Karl's personal Ponzi scheme of robbing Peter to pay Paul and his bookie. Suddenly I realized just how much of a world of difference there was between *comfortable middle-class* and the One Percent.

Zack, on the other hand, appeared unimpressed by the grandeur of this castle on a hill. He had moved into the apartment above my garage to escape the celebrity spotlight of Manhattan. Before we met, he had dated models and actresses, appearing more than once on the pages of *People* magazine, a starlet always on his arm for some gala or opening. He claimed he never wanted anything to do with the A-list life and blamed all of it on a money-hungry publicist with paparazzi on his payroll. Still, I could easily picture him at a cocktail party in this room. I, on the other hand, felt totally out of my element.

I turned from staring at the Renoir as the sound of heels clicking on marble approached. Virginia Owens stepped into the room, took one look at me and all the color drained from her face.

SEVENTEEN

Zack reached for Virginia Owens, taking hold of her elbow to steady her. "Are you all right?" I asked as he led her to the nearest chair.

She quickly regained her composure. Color flooded back into her cheeks, due in part, no doubt, to her embarrassment. She waved away my concern. "I'm fine, thank you. I should know not to skip breakfast, but I was running late this morning and didn't want to keep you waiting."

She extended her right hand. A four-carat marquis diamond sparkled on her ring finger. Her face indicated she frequented a skilled plastic surgeon to stave off the ravages of time, but the crepe-like skin and blue veins lining the back of her hand gave a truer indication of her age. "Virginia Owens," she said. "And you're Anastasia Pollack?"

I nodded. "Should we ask the maid to bring you something?"

"No need. She's already preparing a tray." She turned to Zack. "You probably don't remember me, Mr. Barnes, but we met at a charity auction for the homeless a few years ago. I bid on several of your photographs."

"Did you win the bids?" he asked.

"Of course. They're hanging in my husband's study. I'll show them to you later."

"I'd like that," said Zack.

"I must say, I am rather surprised to see you here," she continued.

"Why is that?"

"Isn't an assignment like this a little beneath your stellar reputation?" She cast a critical eye in my direction, sizing me up as if she were interviewing a prospective servant. Her attitude suggested she found me unworthy of living on the same planet as Zack—and her.

"Would you prefer a staff photographer took your picture?" I asked.

Virginia Owens placed a palm across her breast. "Of course not. I'm honored that Mr. Barnes will be shooting me. I only meant..." Her voice trailed off, and she abruptly changed the subject. "What made you decide to invite me to take part in this story, Mrs. Pollack?"

Time for a not-so-little white lie. "My editorial director suggested you and your husband. She wanted a cross-section of couples, some with recognizable names along with a few average Joes and Janes."

"I see."

The maid returned with a tray holding an antique Paul Revere silver coffee service. A second maid followed with a tray containing silverware, Raynaud Duchesse china, and an assortment of fruits, cheeses, and teacakes. I stole my gaze from the silver and china that loudly proclaimed Virginia Owens never settled for anything but the best. The paintings aside, I could pay off all my debts and live forever in the lap of extreme luxury just from the various antiques in this room.

Yet, if Karl hadn't left me in debt, I never would have met Zack. I suppose there's a reason for everything. We just don't always know what it is at first.

I studied Virginia Owens. From the top of her perfectly coifed and highlighted ash blond—not-a-hair-out-of-place—head, to her Size Four winter-white cashmere slacks and blush silk shirt, to the tips of her gray suede Chanel pumps, she looked like she'd stepped out of the pages of *Town & Country* magazine. Still, I wouldn't trade her life for mine. I've got Zack, and I've got my sons. That makes me the wealthiest pauper in the world.

The maids placed the trays on an eighteenth-century Chippendale sideboard beneath the Monet and proceeded to serve us. I held onto the cup and saucer, worth more than my weekly salary, for dear life. I didn't dare risk balancing a dessert plate on my lap, no matter how yummy those teacakes looked.

"Will your husband be joining us?" I asked. "We did want the male perspective on the importance of maintaining family histories for future generations."

"Unfortunately, he was called away this morning on an important business matter."

Strike two. Or three, considering I'd basically eliminated Coach Renquist from contention. I forced my expression to remain neutral to cover up my disappointment and said, "That's too bad. I was looking forward to meeting him."

Virginia Owens raised an eyebrow. "Why is that?"

"I've never met a real estate tycoon." I smiled as I placed my cup and saucer on the coffee table and pulled out my tape recorder. "Shall we begin the interview?"

She relaxed back in her chair and gestured for me to proceed. After half an hour I had only a smattering of basic information for my article. She asked more questions about me than she answered about herself. Citing privacy concerns, she kept her responses general rather than specific. "We always worry about the possibility of a kidnapping," she explained, even refusing to divulge how she and her husband had met. Did she fear a time-traveling kidnapper?

Still, her concerns didn't prevent her from posing in front of her Monet. In fact, she suggested the shot. I suppose she had more confidence in her hi-tech security system than *American Woman*'s readership. After all, you never know when one of those middle-class housewives might troll an issue in search of a potential ransom candidate.

"May I see your family photos?" I asked, hoping to salvage something from the wasted morning.

"Of course." Virginia Owens placed her dishes on the coffee table and stood. "This way, please."

Zack and I followed her out of the room and across the foyer into a formal dining room with a table large enough to seat a dinner party of thirty-six. Dozens of plastic shoeboxes, labeled by year, covered one end of the table.

"Sometimes I wonder where the years have gone," she said. She sighed as she indicated the boxes with a broad sweep of her arm. "*Tempus fugit*. I always intended to organize our family photos into albums but as you can see, best laid plans...That's why I was thrilled when I learned of your project. I'd like to hire you to organize all of these photos into albums for me."

Lupe had presented me with one small suitcase of old photographs. What confronted me was easily twenty times the number of snapshots.

"What about those?" I pointed to several old photo albums stacked alongside the boxes.

She picked up the top album and flipped it open to the first page, one that contained deckled-edged snapshots of a newborn Albert Owens, the photos attached with old-fashioned corner mounts to a black construction paper page. His name and date of birth were written in delicate white ink script at the top of the page. "These are from my husband's childhood. I thought you might like to see them."

Zack took a few shots of Virginia flipping through the pages of her husband's early years. "Do you have any albums from your childhood?" I asked.

"My mother has them. My husband's parents are deceased." She closed the album and turned to face me. "I know I'll never get around to organizing all these photos, and my children will never forgive me if I die without doing so. I'm willing to pay you well, Mrs. Pollack."

Given my precarious financial situation, I found it impossible to turn down any form of moonlighting, no matter how daunting the task. "Are the individual photos labeled?"

"I believe some are. It's been years since I've looked at any of them."

"I'd need you to do some preliminary work."

She frowned. "How much work?"

"Sort through each box. Pull the photos you'd like included in the albums, and write any missing names and dates on the backs."

Virginia Owens directed her frown toward the stack of boxes.

"I don't know that I'll have the time before I leave."

"You've waited this long. A few more months won't matter." I fished a business card from my purse and handed it to her. "Once you've culled the photos, get in touch with me. At that point I'll be able to give you an estimate of the cost."

She glanced at the card before placing it in her pants pocket. "That sounds fair."

A few minutes later Zack and I departed the Owens estate. Nothing I had learned brought me any closer to discovering the identity of the man who had raped Carmen or whether someone had targeted Lupe. That left one interview—State Assemblyman Mickey Rigato and his wife. Given my success rate so far, I wasn't at all optimistic I'd fair any better with them.

We were meeting the assemblyman and his wife at his district office on Stuyvesant Ave. in Union. However, minutes after Zack pulled onto Rt. 78 the assemblyman's secretary phoned to reschedule the appointment.

"He had to rush off to Trenton for an emergency budget meeting," I told Zack after I hung up from the call. "His secretary said he and his wife can meet me at their home in Cranford at six this evening as long as the interview won't exceed an hour. They have a dinner engagement later tonight."

"Do you want to head home?" asked Zack. "Or should I drop you at the magazine for a few hours?"

"You'd have to pick me up later."

"I don't mind. My calendar is clear."

I loved Zack for his willingness to sit in rush hour traffic for me, but I'd bank the offer for some day in the future when I really needed to call in a favor. "I'm already scheduled to be out of the office all day. Let's go home. With Lucille cooling her tootsies in a cell and the boys in school, we'll have the house to ourselves."

Zack turned to me and raised an eyebrow. "Is that a proposition, Mrs. Pollack?"

"You catch on quickly, Mr. Barnes."

~*~

At six o'clock that evening Zack and I arrived at the Rigato home, an understated early twentieth century Craftsman a few miles from my own house. If the payoff rumors were true, the assemblyman certainly hadn't channeled the graft he accepted into an over-the-top McMansion. The house, situated on a tree-lined street of similarly modest early nineteen-hundreds homes, certainly didn't stand out in any way from the other homes on the street.

Mickey Rigato answered the door after I rang the bell. Although not the kind of man who would stand out in a crowd—balding gray head, average height, and in need of shedding twenty or thirty pounds—I recognized him immediately. Once every two years for as long as I'd lived in Westfield, he's shown up on my doorstep during campaign season. I'd even voted for him on more than one occasion, mostly because throughout my adult life I've found myself staring at a choice between two questionable candidates and eventually pulled the lever for what amounted to the lesser of two evils. At least Mickey Rigato came with a reputation for getting things done.

A true politician, he greeted me as if we were old friends. Cynic that I am, I suspect he'd checked the voter registration roles to ascertain my party affiliation before agreeing to the interview.

After I introduced Zack, he ushered us into a living room furnished in what I recognized as period Stickley pieces in keeping with the style of the house. If the furnishings weren't antiques, they were darned good reproductions. Perhaps that's where he and his wife spent the graft he pocketed—assuming the rumors were true.

Mrs. Rigato, the quintessential gracious politician's wife decked out in a pale pink twin sweater set and a delicate strand of pearls, rose from the sofa to greet us. "Would you join us in a glass of wine?" she asked, nodding to a bottle of pinot grigio and four glasses at the ready on the coffee table.

"Thank you." Zack and I took seats in the two easy chairs on the opposite side of the coffee table.

Mrs. Rigato handed the bottle and a corkscrew to her husband. "Will you do the honors, dear?" While he uncorked the wine, she turned back to me and said, "We're delighted you've invited us to take part in your article. I must admit, though, I'm a bit of a slacker when it comes to keeping up with family photos."

"You must not be a complete slacker," I said, nodding to the stack of five or six albums perched on the end of the coffee table.

She laughed. "Those are from the early years of our marriage and filled mostly with pictures of our children, but as the years went by, for some reason I took less and less photos."

"That's quite common," I said. Zack flipped open the top album and took a few shots as I continued. "Most people have album upon album of snapshots of their first child. By the time the last one comes along, it's Christmas, birthdays, and the yearly school photos. Sometimes a few pictures to document a special family vacation or event but little else."

"I wonder why that is," she said, passing around glasses of wine as her husband poured. "It's not that we loved our younger children any less."

"No, of course not," I said, "but the more children we have, the less time there is to spread among them. We're always running, juggling all sorts of commitments and rarely think to grab the camera to document our daily lives."

"Yet now we always have our cameras with us," said Assemblyman Rigato. He pulled his phone from his pocket and held it up. "Taking photos has never been easier. No film and flash bulbs to buy, no trips to the drug store to drop off film for developing and printing. And people document all sorts of things these days, many that should never be captured for posterity, let alone shared with the world on social media."

The four of us laughed.

"That's the paradox," said Zack.

"People are taking more photos, thanks to smart phones," I said. "My concern—and the reason for my article—is that all those snapshots can easily disappear. Phones die. Most people don't think to back up their files. Or they either don't want to pay for cloud storage or forget to renew their subscription. Others don't think to share storage information with a trusted family member. When they die, their heirs can't access their virtual albums."

Mrs. Rigato took a small sip of her wine. "I never thought of that."

"Your generation, and those who came before you, had actual snapshots," I said, "whether they were stored in shoeboxes in a closet, mounted in albums, or framed and displayed in their homes. My fear is that too many future generations will never have a pictorial record of their families because we now rely too much on Facebook and Instagram. What happens if one day they go the way of the dodo bird?"

"Highly unlikely, don't you think?" asked Assemblyman

Rigato.

"Is it?" I asked. "Companies go out of business all the time. Technology becomes obsolete. Think of all the people who have home movies on VHS tapes or files on floppy disks."

"But there are companies that will convert those files," he said.

"For now. But many people never get around to converting their files. Besides, someday that conversion equipment will no longer exist. A hundred years from now when your great-great-great grandson stumbles upon an antique iPhone or a box of CD's in an attic, will he be able to access the photos on them? Probably not. Yet we still have photographic records of the Civil War, thanks to preservation efforts by historians with foresight. I think families should have that same sort of foresight."

I then proceeded to tell them about the suitcase of photos a deceased neighbor's daughter had asked me to preserve for her. Of course, I didn't mention any names. "That's what got me thinking about all of this."

"Why the interviews?" asked Rigato. "Not that I don't welcome positive press."

"Especially in an election year?" I asked.

He punctuated a shrug with a chuckle. "It certainly doesn't hurt."

"The interviews were my editorial director's idea. She thought it would give some gravitas and cachet to the article."

"Showing that people in all walks of life are guilty of the same lack of foresight?" asked Mrs. Rigato.

"Exactly, not to mention that interviews with celebrities and politicians always sell more issues. Most people have a bit of voyeur in them. They love hearing interesting personal stories about famous people."

She glanced at her wristwatch. "Then we'd best get on with the interview. We have a prior engagement."

I pulled the tape recorder from my purse. "Do you mind?"

Neither Mr. nor Mrs. Rigato objected. I depressed the button. "You might find these questions a bit unusual for an article about scrapbooking, but I chose them because I want them to spur our readership into thinking about their own lives, especially important events and friendships from their past. Let's begin with how the two of you met."

Mrs. Rigato blushed. "In the most cliché of ways. I was a poli-sci major in college. The summer going into my senior year I worked as an intern in the State House. Mickey was serving his first term. It was love at first sight."

I peppered the Rigatos with questions about their youth, making certain I asked Mrs. Rigato as many questions as her husband, even though she was of no interest to me.

Having met her husband in college, she'd have no knowledge of what happened the night of the party. After all, what man—especially a politician—would admit taking part in drugging and raping a couple of fourteen-year-olds? If Rigato had a hand in what happened to Elena and Carmen, he'd keep the secret deeply buried. His political career depended on it. Then again, that also gave him motive for trying to silence someone snooping into his past.

However, Mickey Rigato was genuinely a nice guy, or he'd mastered the art of projecting such an image. Stereotypes aside, my money—if I had any—was still on Peter Donatello. The guy had spiked my sleaze-o-meter firmly into the red zone.

"One final question," I said. "So many of us lose touch with friends who meant a great deal to us at some point in our lives.

Could you pick up the phone today and call your childhood best friend?"

The Assemblyman lowered his head and shook it. "I wish. My closest friend overdosed on heroin shortly after we graduated high school." His wife reached over and clasped his hand in both of hers. Rigato raised his head and sighed deeply before continuing in a ragged voice. "My biggest regret in life is that I didn't see the signs, didn't realize the demons he struggled to exorcise. People—men, especially—kept too much buried back then."

Now we were getting somewhere. "What sort of demons?"

Rigato shook his head again. "I'd rather not say. It wouldn't be fair to his family. After Kirk died, it became their secret to share if they so chose." He glanced at his watch, then rose. "I'm sorry, but on that somber note we really do need to bring this interview to an end."

EIGHTEEN

"Sounds like the deceased football player was the rapist," I said as Zack and I drove home. "My money was on Donatello."

"You have no money," he reminded me.

"And that's a good thing. I would have lost a bundle in a bet."

Zack grew thoughtful. "Under the circumstances, this is probably the best outcome," he said.

"How so?"

"If Lupe awakens from her coma, you can give her some closure, but she won't be able to confront her mother's rapist."

"Good point. Given her rage, there's no telling what she may have done."

"It also means the hit-and-run had no connection to Lupe asking questions at the school."

"Right. Poor Lupe was simply in the wrong place at the wrong time. No one was trying to shut her up."

"Exactly."

A few minutes later we walked into the house and were

immediately swarmed by two extremely hyper teenagers before we even had a chance to remove our coats.

"Mom, you're never going to believe what happened," said Alex.

My heart sank. "Lucille made bail?" I suppose it was unrealistic to hope the police would keep her cooling her tootsies behind bars until Monday. I couldn't remember the last time I had a weekend free of Mama, Lucille, or both of them camped out in what used to be Nick's bedroom.

"Worse," said Nick.

I'm not sure what could be worse than my mother-in-law arriving home from her forced stay in the Westfield hoosegow. She'd inevitably blame me for her arrest and make my life miserable for days—if not weeks.

"Remember Matt Ronson?" asked Alex.

"Remember? How could I forget the original Bad Seed?"

Zack raised his eyebrows. "As in a demonic child?"

"Definitely," I said, then went on to explain. "Matt Ronson was in Alex's nursery school class. He moved here mid-year from Chicago. One day Alex was invited to his home after school. When Nick and I drove over to pick Alex up, the kid nearly killed Nick."

"He wrapped his hands around my neck and squeezed," said Nick. Alex started screaming, and Mom came running."

"Thankfully, I was near enough to stop him before Nick passed out," I said. "Needless to say, that was the first and last time Alex had anything to do with Matt Ronson."

"Why would he do such a thing?" asked Zack.

"His mother apologized profusely, saying Matt had been acting hostile ever since they moved."

"Knowing that, she placed another child in jeopardy?"

"Exactly what I said to her. She thought if Matt made some friends, he'd straighten out and start behaving. I was furious."

"What happened to Matt?" asked Zack.

"He got worse," I said. "I later learned his mother had lied to me. The move to New Jersey only exacerbated psychotic tendencies he'd exhibited back in Chicago."

"He stomped his grandmother's canary to death," said Alex. "And he strangled his sister's kitten."

"The mother admitted that?" asked Zack.

"Hardly," I said.

"Matt bragged about it in school," said Alex. "Everyone was afraid of him. One day in second grade he stabbed the class hamster with a pen and was kicked out of school."

"Matt's parents placed him in a school for emotionally disturbed kids," I said. "That was the last I heard about him until now."

"That school didn't help," said Alex.

"What do you mean?" I asked.

"He finally got even with his parents. He torched his house last night."

"My god!" I said. "Was anyone hurt?"

"His parents and sister are in the hospital with smoke inhalation. Matt was arrested."

Being reminded of Matt Ronson got me thinking. What if Cloris and her husband weren't the victims of a scam? What if the buyers really were innocent? Could one or more of their kids have created The Sentinel because they resented being uprooted from the only life they'd ever known and dragged halfway across the country to an unfamiliar town populated by strangers?

Would the police or the private investigator have even thought to question the homebuyers' kids?

"I have to make a phone call," I said, heading to the kitchen. I grabbed the phone and punched in the speed dial for Cloris's number. As soon as she answered, I asked her that very question.

"I don't know," she said. "Probably not. I believe our realtor mentioned they're relatively young."

"How young?"

"Pre-teen, I think."

"Old enough."

"For what?"

"Revenge." I quickly told her about Matt Ronson.

"You think one of the buyers' kids wrote those letters?"

"I think it's certainly worth investigating."

"*I* think I need to get off the phone and call the lawyer."

"Go for it."

~*~

After breakfast the next morning Alex and Nick left for their part-time jobs at Starbucks and Trader Joe's, Zack headed up to his apartment to prepare for an upcoming assignment, and I tackled a week's worth of laundry and various other household chores. I was in the middle of stripping the sheets off my bed when the phone rang. Although the display came up as *Unknown Caller*, the number looked vaguely familiar, so instead of automatically dismissing it as a robocall, I decided to answer. "Hello?"

"Mrs. Pollack, this is Virginia Owens."

Although the business card I had handed her the day before contained both my office and cell numbers, I was surprised to hear from her so soon. "Have you thought of something else you'd like to add to the interview, Mrs. Owens?"

"No, but after you left yesterday, I realized that if I didn't sort through those boxes of photographs now, I'd probably never get to them. I immediately began sorting through several of the oldest ones, choosing and labeling snapshots I'd like included in albums. I've set aside enough for at least two or three albums at this point."

"That must have taken quite some time."

"It did. I stayed up half the night."

She said this as though it were my fault she missed her beauty sleep. "You must be exhausted this morning."

"I am, but that's neither here nor there. I'd like to drop the photos off so you can get started on the albums. I want them finished by the time my husband and I return for Christmas."

"Christmas? That's only a month away."

"Which should give you ample time to assemble two or three albums."

I wanted to remind her I wasn't one of her servants, but I clamped my tongue firmly between my teeth. After all, thanks to Dead Louse of a Spouse, I was in no position to turn away any freelance jobs, especially from someone as rich as Virginia Owens.

"I plan to take the remaining boxes with me when we jet down to our winter home in a few days," she continued. "I'll give you those photos for the other albums when you deliver the first set."

"We haven't discussed the scope of the project or my fee," I reminded her. "How many albums do you have in mind?

"As many as it takes to include all the photos I decide to give you."

"I see, and do you want scrapbooks of the actual snapshots, or do you want me to scan the photos to create printed albums for you?"

"What do you mean by *printed* albums?"

I quickly explained the process. "A huge benefit is once the album is designed, you can order as many copies as you'd like from the company that produces them."

"Why would I want more than one copy?"

"To give to other family members. I'm currently working on one for the daughter of a neighbor who recently died. She discovered a suitcase of old family photos while cleaning out her mother's home and wants albums made for each of her children."

"I see. All right. I'll think about it. We can discuss the details when I drop off the first group of photos."

"You want to come here?" I could just imagine the look on her face when she pulled up to the curb of my mid-century tract rancher in desperate need of a fresh coat of paint, not to mention what she'd say once she stepped inside. Original linoleum covered my kitchen and bathroom floors. My countertops were metal-edged Formica. Mid-century modern might be on-trend right now, but my home wasn't trendy. It was simply worn-out.

Once upon a time, back when I thought I was living the American dream, Karl and I had discussed renovating. Somewhere I even had wood, tile, and granite swatches I'd picked up one day. "I'm not exactly around the corner from you," I said. "I live half an hour away."

"That's not a problem. When would be a good time to meet without us being disturbed?"

"Any time this morning works for me."

"Your address?"

I rattled off my address. "Perfect. I'll see you in about an hour."

Shortly after I tossed the sheets into the wash, I received a text from Zack: Heading out to run some errands. Wait lunch for me.

I responded with a thumbs-up emoji.

~*~

My doorbell rang just as I finished vacuuming a week's worth of dog hair from the living room and dining room carpets. My dream of hardwoods throughout the house having died with Karl, I was stuck with wall-to-wall gold shag installed by the former owners back in the seventies.

I glanced out the window to find a black Mercedes SUV parked at the curb and Virginia Owens standing at my front door. Unseen, I watched her for a few seconds as she scrutinized my peeling paint. Her expression was exactly as I'd imagined it would be. I couldn't wait to see what she thought of my home's interior.

I walked over to the foyer, swung open the door, and invited her inside. "How quaint," she said, her gaze darting around as I directed her into the living room and offered her a seat on the sofa.

"Thank you but I'll remain standing for now," she said. "I'm a bit stiff from sitting in the car."

She wore a mid-length black mink coat and carried a large gray quilted leather Prada tote that coordinated with her ankle boots. She carried no box or large envelope stuffed with photographs. "I thought you were bringing photos."

She patted her Prada. "I have them in here."

I glanced at the tote, barely large enough to hold an oversized envelope, let alone enough snapshots for two or three albums. Perhaps she only wanted one photo displayed on each page. I'd get paid for my time no matter how many or how few pictures filled the album. I gave myself a brain shrug, then asked, "May I take your coat?"

"Thank you, no. I'll keep it on for now."

Maintaining my hostess persona, I asked, "Would you like something to drink?"

"*Let's drink together friendly and embrace. King Henry the Fourth, Part Two*. Act Four, Scene Two."

Virginia jumped. "Who was that? I thought you said you were alone."

"That's just Ralph. He's an African Grey parrot I inherited from my great-aunt."

She eyed me skeptically. "A parrot that quotes Shakespeare?"

"My aunt was a Shakespearean scholar."

Her eyes darted around the room as she clenched the strap of her bag, her knuckles turning white. "Where is he?"

"Don't worry. He's in his cage." I avoided mentioning that Ralph knew how to pick the lock.

She relaxed slightly. "I'm not fond of animals."

Could have fooled me. "So…" I clapped my hands together and steered the conversation away from Ralph. "Would you like a cup of tea? Coffee?"

"Tea, please." She followed me into the kitchen.

I removed a box of teabags from a cabinet and showed it to her. "We're not big tea drinkers. Is this satisfactory?"

Her nose wrinkled. "I suppose it will have to do."

I grabbed a mug, filled it with water, and placed it in the microwave to heat. When I turned around, Virginia Owens was pointing a gun at me.

NINETEEN

At first my brain refused to function. I stared at the gun, then at the woman brandishing it. Although this wasn't the first time someone had pointed a gun at me, I'd never get used to it. However, with the exception of a couple of psycho lovers, the previous threats on my life had come from the Mafia and hired hit men, not mink-clad socialites. I couldn't wrap my head around Virginia Owens wanting to harm me. Was I dealing with another psycho?

"How about if you put the gun away before someone gets hurt?" I said. "We can discuss whatever is bothering you without a weapon."

She laughed. "I don't think so."

At that moment Mephisto, who had been cowering under Lucille's bed while I ran the vacuum, paddled into the kitchen, took one look at Virginia, and began to growl. She waved the gun wildly in his direction. "Get that dog out of here, or I'll shoot him."

"There's no need to shoot. Where would you like me to put

him?"

"I don't care. Lock him up somewhere. I hate dogs."

Mephisto's growl grew deeper. The feeling was obviously mutual. His sudden appearance and Virginia's reaction to him gave me an idea. If I let Mephisto out the back door, Zack would see him when he arrived home and know something was wrong. We never let Mephisto loose in the backyard. He'd invariably eat something he shouldn't, then barf it up once he came back into the house.

I raised my hands up, palms out. "Okay, I'm going to kneel down and grab his collar. I'll put him outside, all right?"

"Just do it. And don't get any ideas."

I ushered Mephisto toward the mudroom. Virginia followed, her gun pressing firmly into the center of my back.

"I'm going to open the back door now," I said.

"Not all the way. Only enough for the mutt to squeeze through. Then shut it."

I did as she directed.

"Now lock it."

I flipped the deadbolt. No matter. Zack had a key.

"Slowly turn around and walk back into the kitchen."

"Why are you doing this?" I asked as I retraced my steps. Once back in the kitchen I positioned myself in such a way that her back faced the window. I didn't want her to see Zack when he arrived home. Hopefully she wouldn't hear his car pulling into the driveway. "What have I ever done to you?"

"You stuck your nose where it didn't belong. Now I have to clean up another mess."

Was she doing this to protect her husband? Was he the rapist, not the football player who had died? Or were both boys responsible? And how the heck did she find out my true motive for arranging the interviews?

One thing I did know: I couldn't disarm Virginia Owens on my own. My only chance of getting out of this alive was to keep her talking until Zack returned, which I hoped was sooner rather than later because right now I didn't know how much of a *later* I had left. "I don't understand."

"Don't play dumb with me."

"I'm not. Honestly, I have no idea why you're holding me at gunpoint. I never met you before yesterday. I don't know anything about you other than what you yourself told me during the interview." Which wasn't much. At times I wondered which one of us was conducting that interview.

"Is that so?"

Wasn't it? I studied the woman holding my life in her hands. "Who *are* you?"

"Someone who got cheated out of her rightful place on the cheerleading squad, thanks to your friend."

Cheerleading squad? "You must have me confused with someone else. Besides, aren't you a little old for cheerleading?"

"I wasn't back in high school. There was one opening for a freshman. That spot was rightfully mine before the cheerleading coach decided we needed to be welcoming to the *immigrant* and chose Elena over me."

Suddenly the puzzle pieces all dropped into place. "And you decided to get even?"

"Damn right, I did."

"You set up Elena and Carmen. You're the football player's sister who invited them to the party."

"Carmen was merely collateral damage. I had nothing against

her."

Talk about cold and heartless! "You drugged them, didn't you?"

"My brother came up with the idea and provided the drugs. After Elena and Carmen passed out, we had the other boys help carry them down to the rec room to sleep it off."

"Except someone went back downstairs and raped Elena and Carmen."

"Elena got what she deserved. She stole from me; my brother stole from her. Quid pro quo."

"Were the other boys involved in the rape?"

She shook her head. "They were too busy getting stoned upstairs to know what was going on downstairs."

"Carmen wound up pregnant."

Virginia shrugged. "That's on Elena, not me. She's the one who insisted on bringing Carmen to the party."

"Your brother died not long afterwards, didn't he?"

"That's on Elena, too."

"How so?"

"He developed a conscience all of a sudden." She said this with a sneer that suggested having a conscience was a bad thing.

"He died of an accidental overdose, didn't he?"

"Not so accidental."

"He committed suicide?"

"That would have been preferable. He was going to admit what we'd done. I couldn't let him do that. He'd ruin my life."

My jaw dropped as I processed Virginia's words. "You murdered your brother?"

"I had no choice. In hindsight I should have just given Elena a lethal dose, but then she wouldn't have suffered, and I wanted her to suffer for what she'd taken from me."

When she shrugged to show her lack of remorse, I knew I was dealing with a psychopath. "How did you find out I was investigating what had happened to Elena and Carmen?"

"I didn't know until you showed up at my house. You shocked the hell out of me when I saw you."

"That bit about not having eaten breakfast, that was all an act?"

"I have a talent for thinking on my feet. I recognized you from the coffee shop. You and that other woman, Carmen's daughter, were sitting with Elena at the table behind me. At first I didn't recognize Elena. I hadn't seen her in decades. Then she started telling you what had happened the night of the party. I knew from Carmen's daughter's reaction that she was going to be trouble. When the two of you left, I followed you."

This all seemed a bit too coincidental. "Cranford is a long way from Bedminster. What were you doing there?"

"I had dropped my mother off at the convent. She spent Thanksgiving with us. I stopped for a cup of coffee before heading home."

"Your mother's a nun?"

"She blamed herself for my brother's death and began spending all her time in church. When my father died from a heart attack a few years later, she decided to dedicate her life to God instead of me. Something else I can blame on Elena. She took my mother from me."

It seemed to me Virginia was the one responsible for all that had happened in her family, but I wasn't about to challenge her cause-and-effect rationalization while she pointed a gun at me.

Where the heck was Zack?

"Carmen's daughter is lying in a coma in the hospital. Are you responsible for that?"

"I hired someone to follow her. When I learned she'd gone to the school and discovered the names of the football players, I had to keep her from contacting my husband. It cost me a fortune."

"He killed one woman and seriously injured two others."

"He botched the job. He killed the wrong woman. I'm going to have to do something about that if she ever wakes up."

"You won't get away with this," I told her.

"I already have. For fifty years. I'm not going to let a few loose ends get in my way now."

"I have security cameras. The police will look at the footage and see you entering my home."

She laughed. "I wasn't born yesterday. You expect me to believe a dump like this has security cameras?"

"Laugh all you want, but you'll be laughing behind bars. There's a camera pointed at my front door and another pointed at the street in front of my house. My body will still be warm when you're arrested for my murder."

Virginia hesitated for a split second before recovering and saying, "You're bluffing."

"Am I? Is that a chance you're willing to take?"

"Prove it." She grabbed my arm and dragged me from the kitchen toward the front door. "Open the door, and show me the cameras."

As we approached the foyer, out of the corner of my eye I spied Ralph flying through the house, making a beeline—or in this case, a parrot-line—directly toward the fur-draped Virginia. He swooped onto Virginia's sleeve and yanked a beak full of mink from the coat.

Virginia let loose a bloodcurdling scream, released her grip on me, and flayed her arms wildly. Having gotten what he wanted, Ralph flew off and perched on a lampshade in the living room. Virginia pointed the gun at Ralph, then at me, then back toward Ralph, all the while continuing to scream incoherently.

"Get that...that thing out of here," she finally yelled at me, waving the gun. Ralph took flight. Virginia fired off a round as he headed our way. The bullet took out my lamp. As Ralph flew over us, another bullet whizzed past my ear. Ralph headed down the hallway toward the bedrooms. Virginia's next shot pierced the wall.

I had to stop her before one of those bullets wound up in me. As she pivoted away from me to fire off another round down the hallway, I hurled myself at her back. I outweighed her by at least thirty pounds, and she went down with a thud, another bullet flying from the gun as she hit the floor. But cushioned by her fur coat, the force of the tackle didn't even knock the wind out of her, and worse yet, she maintained a fierce grip on the gun.

For a sixty-five-year-old Size Four, Virginia Owens was surprisingly strong. She probably spent her days working out with a personal trainer named Sven. I grabbed for her wrists, wrapping my fingers around them, fighting to keep the gun pointed away from me, as we rolled around on the floor.

She kicked at me with little success. Her mink coat encumbered her and cushioned any blows she managed to land. However, the coat didn't hamper her teeth as she sank them into my arm directly above my wrist, drawing blood. With my other arm I tried to elbow her in the jaw while still maintaining my grip on her wrists, but she only clenched down harder. I swear she struck bone. Excruciating pain radiated up my arm. Black spots danced before my eyes.

And then I saw a man's foot stamp down hard on Virginia's wrist, the one connected to the hand that held the gun. She screamed so loudly in my ear I went deaf for a moment. The next thing I knew Zack had Virginia pinned to the floor, his knee on her back, her gun firmly in his hand and pointed at her head.

"Get off me!" she screamed.

"Not a chance, lady."

She twisted her neck until she could get a look at Zack. Realizing who had restrained her, her jaw dropped. "You! What the hell are *you* doing here?"

"He lives here," I said.

Before she could respond, Ralph flew back into the foyer. Settling on the floor inches from Virginia's face, he flapped his wings and stared at her.

"Get that vile thing away from me!" she shrieked.

"I don't think so." I turned to Zack. "She tried to kill Ralph. Looks like he's taking a bit of revenge."

Ralph squawked in agreement. "*Blood and revenge are hammering in my head. Titus Andronicus.* Act Five, Scene Ten." Then he planted his beak into her fur collar.

"You go, Ralph," I said.

Virginia cringed, her entire body shuddering as she tried without success to inch herself away from him.

"You okay?" Zack asked me as Ralph continued to peck at Virginia's coat and she continued to scream.

I dragged myself across the foyer and propped my back against the wall, cradling my injured arm in my lap. Blood dripped from the puncture wounds. Good thing vampires only exist in fiction. "I'll live, but I'd better get a tetanus shot."

~*~

Zack and I watched as Officers Harley and Fogarty hauled Virginia Owens from my house toward their police cruiser.

"I don't think we need to call an ambulance for your wound," said Detective Spader, pointing to my arm, "but I want you checked out at the hospital. I'll have one of the other officers drive you."

"No need," said Zack. "I'll take her."

Spader nodded. "I'm going to hold you to that."

"Really, Detective," I said. "There's no point in spending taxpayer dollars."

Spader turned back to me. "Don't think I won't check up on you."

"Scout's honor." I held up my uninjured arm and formed my fingers into the Girl Scout pledge sign. "We'll lock up the house and drive directly to the hospital."

He nodded before heading to his car.

"That's one seriously evil woman," I said as Zack and I watched the patrol car carrying Virginia Owens pull away from the curb. "I wonder if her mother suspected Virginia killed her brother."

As we stepped back into the house, and Zack closed the door behind us, he asked, "Why do you say that?"

I quickly caught Zack up on everything Virginia had divulged to me. "I suppose spilling her murderous secrets didn't matter since she planned to kill me. Dead craft editors tell no tales."

"You think her mother may have known what happened the night of the party? Weren't the parents out of town that night?"

"Yes, but what if the mother overheard Virginia and Kirk arguing over Kirk wanting to confess to what they'd done? Then Kirk supposedly dies of an accidental drug overdose? I don't think someone all of sudden turns into a psychopath. I'll bet Virginia was the kind of kid who stomped canaries and strangled kittens."

"Like Matt Ronson?"

"Exactly."

"Wouldn't her mother have said something if she suspected her daughter killed her son?"

"Not necessarily. Mothers are often in denial when it comes to their children's antisocial behavior."

Zack nodded. "You did say Matt Ronson's mother made excuses and covered up his actions for as long as possible."

"Think about it: Virginia's mother had already lost her son. Then her husband died suddenly. Her crazy daughter was all she had left. Perhaps she joined the convent as penance because she blamed herself for Virginia's actions."

"Because she wasn't a good enough mother?"

"Right. And if so, how could she turn Virginia in to the police if she blamed herself for what Virginia had done? In her mind her only recourse was to absolve herself and her daughter by dedicating the rest of her life to God and prayer."

Zack scowled. "Nun or no nun, if she knows what happened to Carmen and Elena, she's also indirectly responsible for the three victims of the hit-and-run."

"Not only that. For all we know, Virginia may have had something to do with her father's death. What if he also suspected Virginia killed Kirk and confronted her? She could have silenced him in such a way that it looked like a coronary. If the man had a heart condition, no one would have suspected foul play."

"Except her mother."

Another theory crossed my mind. "Maybe her mother joined the convent to keep Virginia from killing her."

"Except they've maintained a relationship. You mentioned

they spent Thanksgiving together."

"It could be an extremely strained relationship for the sake of appearances. Or perhaps her mother now suffers from dementia and has forgotten what happened half a century ago."

The possibilities were endless, and it would take a team of detectives to get to the bottom of it. Detective Spader had taken preliminary statements from Zack and me at the house, but he'd requested we come into headquarters to give signed statements. I'd certainly present my theories to him at that time.

Virginia Owens had the kind of money to buy herself the best defense attorneys in the country. She had known enough to remain silent and stone-faced throughout her arrest, refusing to answer any questions or defend herself against my accusations, even before Detective Spader Mirandized her. Instead, she offered nothing more than a tight-lipped glare—at Detective Spader, at the other cops, and especially at me.

I knew she'd lawyer up immediately, refusing to admit anything during her interrogation. Everything she'd confessed to me boiled down to her word against mine at this point, but I'd do whatever I could to make sure she spent the rest of her life behind bars.

"Let's get you over to the hospital," said Zack.

I'd put on a brave face for Zack and Detective Spader, but my arm throbbed from the excruciating pain. Blood continued to trickle from the holes left by Virginia's teeth. Originally, I planned to clean and bandage the wound myself, but Spader was right. I needed to go to the hospital.

Spader must have called in some favors or pulled a few strings because as soon as we arrived at the hospital, I was ushered into an examination room even though dozens of people filled the emergency waiting room. The attending physician confirmed the seriousness of my injury when after cleaning the puncture wound, he gave me a local and set about stitching me back together. "You're lucky there's no nerve damage," he said.

After bandaging my arm, he capped off my visit with a tetanus shot and a prescription for painkillers. Pain or no pain, though, we were at the hospital, and I wanted to stop by to see Lupe.

"You sure you're up to this?" asked Zack, draping his arm around my shoulders as we stepped into an elevator. "You seem a bit woozy."

I pressed the button for the Intensive Care Unit and smiled at Zack. "I've got you to catch me if I faint."

A moment later the elevator arrived at the designated floor, and the doors opened. Zack swept his free arm in front of us. "As Ralph would say, '*Lead on, Macduff.*'"

"You need to brush up your Shakespeare. Ralph would never misquote The Bard."

His brows knit together in puzzlement. "Isn't that a line from *Macbeth*?"

I shook my head. "The correct wording is '*Lay on, Macduff.*'"

"Hmm...I may be smarter than a fifth grader, but I'm obviously not smarter than a parrot."

I laughed through my pain. "Few people are when it comes to Ralph and Shakespeare."

By then we had arrived at Lupe's room. When I turned to peer through the glass, my jaw dropped.

TWENTY

We found Lupe sitting up in bed, her husband holding her hand. I ran to the door and pushed it open. "You're awake!"

She smiled. She was still hooked up to a myriad of blinking and beeping machines, but her bruises had begun to fade from deep purple to a yellowish green, and although an incredibly sickly color, it indicated her flesh was in the process of healing. "That I am," she said. "A bit the worse for wear but alive and awake."

"With no permanent brain damage," added Andrew.

Lupe frowned. "I was lucky, unlike the other two women who were struck."

"The second woman died late last night," said Andrew. "And the police still haven't caught the bastard responsible."

Zack and I exchanged a knowing glance that didn't go unnoticed by Lupe. "What is it?" she asked. "Don't just stand there in the doorway. Come into the room."

"I thought we weren't allowed," I said. "Immediate family only."

"You need to sit down," Zack said to me. "Forget the rules." He ushered me into the room toward the empty chair on the opposite side of the bed from where Andrew sat, then took up a position behind me.

That's when Lupe noticed my bandage. "What happened to your arm?"

"I was bitten."

"By your mother-in-law's dog?"

I shook my head. "Devil Dog is all bark, no bite. I was attacked by the person who hired the van driver who tried to kill you."

Andrew's jaw dropped. "Are you saying the hit-and-run was deliberate?"

"Was it my mother's rapist?" asked Lupe.

"Not exactly." I leaned forward and placed my hand on her shoulder. "How much do you remember from before the accident?"

"I remember sitting in the coffee shop and Elena telling us about the rape, but everything after that is a total blank."

"The doctors said her memory might return with time," said Andrew, "but there's no guarantee."

I nodded. "You don't remember going to Our Lady of Peace to view a copy of the yearbook?"

She shook her head.

"Someone else was in that coffee shop and overhead Elena, someone who had a vested interest in making sure you didn't find out who had raped your mother that night. She followed you home."

Andrew and Lupe gripped each other's hand so tightly their knuckles turned white. Andrew's entire body stiffened with rage. "Who?"

I took a deep breath and filled them in on everything that had transpired over the last few days, culminating with Virginia showing up at my house this morning. When I finished, they both sat in stunned disbelief. Finally, Lupe said, "All because she didn't make the cheerleading squad?"

"Hard to believe, isn't it?" I said.

"Was she born evil?" asked Lupe. "Or did something happen to her to turn her into a psychopath?"

"We may never know," said Zack.

"Unless she confesses," I said, "but I don't see that happening."

Andrew's face grew purple with rage. "You mean there's a chance she'll get off?"

"I don't think so," said Zack. "My guess is that after the police get a search warrant, they'll find evidence that leads them to the van driver she hired. They'll offer him a deal to rat her out. In addition, if her brother and father weren't cremated, they'll exhume the bodies and look for evidence of murder. And don't forget, she tried to kill Anastasia today. The prosecutor might not be able to convict her on all counts, but he should be able to get her on enough to lock her up for the rest of her life."

"I certainly hope so," said Andrew.

Lupe had grown very quiet. Her features took on a distant quality, as if she'd withdrawn from this world into some remote place no one else could enter. "Lupe?" I squeezed her shoulder and whispered, "Are you all right?"

"I'm trying to fit the puzzle pieces together. The woman responsible for this…Virginia?"

"Owens," I said. "She's married to Albert Owens, the real estate developer. He was one of the football players at the party."

"And she and her brother cooked up that vile scheme together?

211

To punish my mother and aunt?"

"She only wanted to get even with your aunt. She referred to your mother as collateral damage."

"That's a war term," said Lupe. "If she was at war with my aunt, why would she invite her to a party?"

"It was a one-sided war. Elena had no idea Virginia hated her."

"Then why did her brother also rape Mami?"

"Opportunity."

"That makes Virginia Owens my sister's aunt."

Andrew's eyes widened in alarm. "Where are you going with this, Lupe?"

Lupe ignored his question, instead keeping her attention focused on me. "You said she's a psychopath."

"I'm no psychiatrist, but I think it's a good assumption, given everything she did."

"A psychopath and a possible serial killer," said Zack.

"And her brother?" asked Lupe.

"If he wasn't also a psychopath, the creep was probably at least a sociopath," I said.

"Or possibly just a very weak individual easily manipulated by his sister," said Zack.

Lupe bit down on her lower lip and grew silent again. Finally she asked, "Are psychotic tendencies something people can inherit?"

Were they? I had no idea. I looked to Zack for help. His brain contained a vast amount of knowledge on all sorts of topics.

He shrugged. "I don't know. Could be nurture, could be nature."

"Sex offenders were often sexually abused as children," I said. "So maybe the same is true with psychotic behavior."

"If it's nature," said Lupe, "that would mean my sister might carry those crazy genes."

I nodded. "Possibly. But if not, she might be a wonderful, stable person. You have no way of knowing."

"And chances are I'll never know." Lupe closed her eyes and took a deep breath before letting loose a forlorn sigh. "Either way, I think I should forget about trying to find her. The best gift I could possibly give my sister is to spare her the knowledge of her conception."

"I think that's a good idea," said Andrew.

~*~

"That was a difficult decision for Lupe to make," I said as Zack and I headed home. Lupe would have liked to make her mother's rapist pay for what he'd done, but she knew that would never happen. From the beginning I believed what drove her was the possibility of a miraculous reunion with the half-sister she never knew.

My cell phone rang as Zack crossed over from Mountainside into Westfield. I glanced at the display. When I saw that it was Cloris calling, I answered. "Hi."

"You're an absolute genius," she said.

"I am?"

"You solved The Sentinel mystery."

"I did?"

"You were right. The private investigator discovered the new owners' fourteen-year-old son wrote those letters. They're mortified. They can't stop apologizing."

"Probably because they don't want you suing them."

"I'm sure. They've withdrawn the lawsuit and offered to pay all the legal expenses we incurred. Plus, they've offered additional money for our pain and suffering. We owe you big time."

"Hey, what are friends for? You did save my life once, remember?"

"I did, didn't I?"

"How could you forget? Anyway, to quote Ralph, all's well that ends well."

Except as Zack turned onto our street, I realized all wasn't well. Harriet Kleinhample's VW minibus sat parked in front of my house. I groaned. This could mean only one thing: our Lucille reprieve had come to an end. "Well, it was nice while it lasted," I said.

ANASTASIA'S SCRAPBOOKING TIPS

Because of the fragile quality of the photographs Lupe discovered in her mother's attic, Anastasia decided to create a digital scrapbook that could be uploaded to a commercial photo site and printed into a bound album. Printed albums are also great when you want to produce multiple copies of an album for family members.

However, with the wide variety of tools and embellishments available in craft stores, you might want to opt for creating one-of-a-kind scrapbooks. If so, make sure you only use archival quality products that won't discolor your photos over time.

Whether you decide to design a digital album to print or a one-of-a-kind album, keep these tips in mind for the best results:

1. Decide on the theme for your album. You can create an album to commemorate a specific event, such as a birthday or vacation,

or a series of chronological albums that span your family's history.

2. Choose a focal-point photograph for each page. Create a layout for the page by adding other photos that are part of that page's "story."

3. Always keep in mind that "less is more." Too many snapshots on one page will look cluttered. Choose no more than three or four of the most representational photos to highlight.

4. Whether you're choosing backgrounds from a digital site or actual scrapbook pages, make sure the printed patterns and colors don't overpower your photos. The photographs are the stars of your album. Backgrounds are meant to enhance, not steal the show.

5. Use page accents, whether digital artwork or purchased embellishments, sparingly. As with backgrounds, you don't want the embellishments to take over the page. You want your photos to stand out. One embellishment per page every few pages is sufficient.

6. Create a title for pages that represent special events.

7. Note the names of each person in a photo, the year or date, and where the photo was taken. Even though you recognize the people in the photos, years from now you may not, and your descendents certainly won't know their names.

8. If you choose to combine photographs with journaling, make

certain your spelling is correct.

9. Don't go overboard adding lots of catchy quotes or song lyrics.

10. Remember that you're creating a family heirloom that will be viewed by future generations. Don't editorialize by adding disparaging comments about Aunt Irma or Cousin Tiffany.

ABOUT THE AUTHOR

USA Today and Amazon bestselling and award-winning author Lois Winston writes mystery, romance, romantic suspense, chick lit, women's fiction, children's chapter books, and nonfiction under her own name and her Emma Carlyle pen name. *Kirkus Reviews* dubbed her critically acclaimed Anastasia Pollack Crafting Mystery series, "North Jersey's more mature answer to Stephanie Plum." In addition, Lois is an award-winning craft and needlework designer who often draws much of her source material for both her characters and plots from her experiences in the crafts industry. Learn more about Lois and her books, where to find her on social media, and a link for signing up for her newsletter at www.loiswinston.com.

Made in the USA
Monee, IL
08 December 2022